# The
# APPLE TART
## of
# HOPE

# *The* APPLE TART *of* HOPE

## Sarah Moore Fitzgerald

Holiday House / New York

Text copyright © 2014 by Sarah Moore Fitzgerald
Illustrations copyright © 2014 by Leo Nickolls
All Rights Reserved
First published in Great Britain in 2014 by Orion Children's Books.
The rights of Sarah Moore Fitzgerald and Leo Nickolls to be identified as the Author
and Illustrator respectively of the Work have been asserted by them in accordance
with the Copyright, Designs and Patents Act 1988.

HOLIDAY HOUSE is registered in the U.S. Patent and Trademark Office.
Printed and Bound in December 2015 at Maple Press, York, PA, USA.
www.holidayhouse.com
First American Edition
1 3 5 7 9 10 8 6 4 2

Library of Congress Cataloging-in-Publication Data

Names: Fitzgerald, Sarah Moore, 1965- author.
Title: The apple tart of hope / by Sarah Moore Fitzgerald.
Description: First American edition. | New York : Holiday House, 2016. |
Summary: Oscar Dunleavy, a teenager who used to make incredible apple tarts, has
gone missing and everyone thinks he is dead, but Oscar's best friend Meg, and his
little brother Stevie, try to figure out what happened to him and form a bond and
learn about commitment and friendship. | "First published in Great Britain 2014 by
Orion Children's Books."
Identifiers: LCCN 2015022313 | ISBN 9780823435616 (hardcover)
Subjects: | CYAC: Missing children—Fiction. | Hope—Fiction. | Friendship—Fiction.
Classification: LCC PZ7.F5762 Ap 2016 | DDC [Fic]—dc23 LC record available at
HYPERLINK "http://lccn.loc.gov/2015022313" http://lccn.loc.gov/2015022313

*For Ger*

# the first slice

They had to have an ambulance outside the church in case someone fainted. Men with green armbands directed the traffic. Someone had written "FULL" in red on a sign and hung it on the entrance to the car park. Neighbors opened their gates.

Inside, big strips of paper had been taped to the backs of the first four rows of seats on which another sign said, "Reserved for 3R" because only the people in his class were allowed to sit there.

Everyone looked dazed. It was the Day of Prayer for Oscar Dunleavy, who was missing, presumed dead—and no one ever gets used to something like that.

Father Frank was at the absolute center of everything. He said that Oscar's classmates were going to need space and protection and respect on account of the "unnatural, wretched, disbelieving things" you feel when a person in your class looks like they are never going to be seen again.

We were also going to need blankets because the heating in the church had broken down just when the February weather had taken another turn for the worse.

I heard Father Frank talking to the parents about how we were "in for a very difficult time"—facing Oscar's empty desk, and passing his still-padlocked, graffitied locker that nobody had had the heart to wrench open. Father Frank was in his element, focusing on something more important than his usual duties, which normally involved going around the school telling people to pick up their rubbish or to spit out their chewing gum.

Now he was soothing people who were sad and traumatized, and talking a language of grief and comfort that it turns out he is fluent in.

He explained that even when it looked as if everyone was fine, we were going to encounter bewildering moments when the loss of Oscar would be like an assault on our impressionable young minds, not only during these empty sad weeks, but for many years to come.

Everybody filed in. Pale faces. Blotchy red noses. The whole class melded into one single silent smudge, a blue blur of uniforms shimmering like a giant ghost.

Every time I looked at the crowd, I saw something I didn't want to see: a grown man's face quivering, a woman rustling in her bag for a tissue, tears dropping off the end of someone's chin. There were low murmured hellos and unnatural-sounding coughs.

And then there was Oscar's dad, pushing Stevie's wheelchair, the two of them looking like the broken links of a chain. For a second, the squeal of someone's baby drifted above us—an accidental happy little noise ringing out, clear and pure in the middle of the despair. There were flowers, tons and tons of flowers, all blue and yellow.

"Cornflower. Buttercup," said Father Frank somewhere in the middle of his endless speech.

"Cornflower for the blue of his blue eyes. Buttercup for his bright soul." Seriously, that's actually what he said.

There was something in the air that smelled of herbs and musk.

Dust seemed to rise from corners of the church like an unearthly kind of mist. And for the duration of this unwanted ceremony, everyone in my class seemed to be trying their best not to look into each other's eyes.

I was on the verge of assuming that Father Frank's speech really was going to go on forever, but then his voice got deeper and slower and more solemn, signaling the end of something and the beginning of something else.

"Ahem," he said, "now we're going to ask Oscar's best friend to come forward, please, for her reading. She was the person closest to Oscar. She is going to say a few words in memory of her friend—on behalf of all of us who knew him and loved him so well."

I could feel myself heating up with that embarrassment you get when you're not prepared for something important. Nobody had said anything to me about a reading. I wasn't in the mood to stand up in front of anyone or say anything. But I took a couple of deep breaths and I told myself that I had to keep it together for Oscar. I felt sure that the words I was supposed to read would be up there on the stand beside Father Frank, waiting for me. Someone was meant to have cleared this with me in advance, and there must have been a mix-up because nobody had, but I guessed that was probably understandable under the distressing circumstances.

Nobody was hovering nearby waiting to give me instructions, and all I could see was the top of everyone's heads. I got to my feet as the silence bulged inside the church and people shifted around on the benches. The crowd seemed to quiver in front of me.

And then she stood up. Golden-haired and glittery, rising like an angel from her seat and walking so gracefully to the top of the church that it looked as if she was floating. At the sight of her, I was thick-footed—stuck to the floor. The angel girl proceeded to the microphone.

"Who is that?" I asked my mum, who did not know.

"Who"— I leaned over to Andy Fewer who was sitting in the row in front of me—"is that?" And as the girl began to speak I realized that I'd seen the outline of her before and I did know who she was.

*"Death is nothing at all . . ."*

Her voice was like melted chocolate and it drifted among us, as if music had begun to play.

*". . . one brief moment and everything will be as it was before."*

Andy turned to me with a mystified look.

"That's Paloma," he said as if I'd asked him what planet we were on. "Paloma Killealy."

Of course, I thought. Of course it's her.

When she'd finished the reading, she said there was this song that was Oscar's favorite, like, ever, and how whenever she heard it, she'd always think of him.

"This is for you, Osc," she said, and she started to sing some song that I did not recognize.

Osc? Since when was that his name? Nobody ever called him that.


When something bad happens to someone young, and when people get together in a church to say prayers for that person, there is a weird vibration, sort of like a buzz or a whistle. Everything shudders, like I reckon it would at the beginning of an earthquake, as if even the ground is shocked and horrified by the wrongness of it all.

*"There should have been so much time ahead of him,"* was the kind of obvious, useless thing that everyone kept repeating, not that anything anyone said was going to make a single bit of difference—at least not now. It was too late, they said. Because Oscar had made his

decision, and we were going to have to suffer for the rest of our lives because of it. He was gone. And by now, everyone more or less took it for granted that he wasn't coming back.

February had been Oscar's favorite time of the year.

I'd told him he must be the only person in the universe with a pet month, but he was quite stubborn about it. He explained that when you stop being a kid, Christmas is nothing but a terrible disappointment. And January has never been anything but a dark and boring month full of homework and dull dinners. But then, right at that moment when the world seems to be at its bleakest, February creeps up on you like a best friend you haven't seen in a while, tapping you on the shoulder.

Plus, this particular February had been holding up a new sign, allowing us to make plans to do things that none of us had ever done before—exciting stuff— different stuff—teenage stuff. We weren't little kids anymore and this February had been full of a hundred different kinds of new chances.

Now, any of the chances Oscar might ever have had, had dropped radically. To nil.

Outside, on the steps of the church it was formal and hushed, but there was a low murmur that felt as if it was growing, like some distant, gigantic monster was moving closer by the second.

A group of parents clustered around Father Frank, and the sun shone like a cruel joke, making everything seem more beautiful than it deserved to be. Andy was there, and so was Greg, and Father Frank was asking, "Deary, deary me, boys, why? Why would someone with so much going for him have . . . have . . . ended it all in the way he appears to have done?"

"Oh Father, you see, it could be for any number of reasons," Andy said, serious and fluent, as if he was an expert on the subject. "Personally, I think that it's pretty much a miracle that any of us survives."

"What do you mean?" said the priest.

"I mean," continued Andy, "there's this one moment as you're growing up when the world suddenly feels more or less pointless— when the terribleness of reality lands on you, like something falling from the sky."

"Something falling? Like what?" asked Father Frank, trying his best.

"Something big, like a piano, say, or a fridge. And when that happens, there's no going back to the time when it hadn't landed on you."

"But what about the pleasure and the joy and the purpose, like sports, music, girls, and the like?" Father Frank was nearly pleading now.

"Fiction," sighed Andy. "Mirages in the desert of life, to make people feel like it might be worth it."

"Oh," said Father Frank. "Oh I see, and do all you youngsters get this feeling?"

"Yes, I think so," said Andy, not even asking anyone else for their opinion, "but most of us learn to live with it."

"Well that's a relief, I suppose."


It took me ages to find Stevie, who was sitting close to the church entrance in his wheelchair. His dad was nearby, fully occupied with the sober, repetitive job of shaking hundreds of hands.

"Oh Stevie," I said, and I leaned over to hug him and I closed my eyes and the tears that I'd been trying to keep inside came tumbling out.

"It's okay, Meg," he whispered, even though obviously it wasn't. But I felt something a little like relief when I got a chance to look at his face properly. "When did you get back?" he asked, and I told him we'd been back since the night before. That we'd come as quickly as we could, as soon as we'd heard the news. It occurred to me that part of the reason everything felt so wobbly was because I must still be jet-lagged. I couldn't see straight.

But surrounded by this fog of grief, there was a gladness in Stevie, a light in his eyes that lifted my heart slightly, and made me feel that maybe there was some reason to be cheerful, or hopeful, or even faintly optimistic.

"What happened, Stevie? What on earth happened? And why is everyone acting like this? This mass? A *mass*? I mean, you're not supposed to do that unless it's completely clear that the person you're having it for is definitely dead. Not unless there's proof. I mean, there's no reason for us to believe he's *dead*. Is there?"

Stevie looked up at me and swiveled a little closer.

"Exactly!" he whispered. "That's what I've been trying to tell everyone! Thank goodness you're home, Meg, because seriously, you're the first person, the first person I've talked to—apart from myself—who doesn't believe it. I knew I'd be able to count on you and I'm *so* completely glad you've come back, because basically I felt on my own here, kinda thought I was going mad to be honest. Everyone's going around saying he committed suicide. I mean seriously, right? That doesn't make any sense—it really doesn't."

"Stevie, you've got to tell me everything you know. Every single thing that happened before he disappeared."

"I'll do my best, Meg," Stevie said. "I've been going over everything again and again in my head. There's no time to talk now, though," and Stevie frowned and looked around, and he sounded much older and wiser than a kid his age usually sounds. "Let's meet at the pier later on. I'll see you there. Leave it till about midnight, okay?"

"How are you going to get there on your own at that time of night, Stevie?"

"No problemo," he said, in a definitely non-grieving tone, which kept giving me hope. "A lot has happened since you've been gone. I'm practically self-sufficient!" He grinned so widely that he started to attract some unwanted attention, so he changed his expression to something more grave, and, speaking with the furtive confidence of a spy, he told me to mingle, to say nothing and to meet him later as instructed.

The crowd milled. Arms were put around people and there was a lot more crying. Off in the distance every so often I glimpsed the golden hair of Paloma Killealy, and everywhere within the murmuring crowd I seemed to hear her name spoken softly from person to person as if it were a poem. Paloma Killealy. Paloma Killealy. Paloma, Paloma Killealy.

# the second slice

I didn't die. I never died. I'm not dead. Okay, I feel pretty rotten about the whole situation—the way I disappeared that night without saying where I was going and how everyone assumed I really was dead, and the way I let them believe it.

Things had got on top of me. It was because of this whole sequence of events that made me want to cycle faster than I'd ever cycled before down to the shore and tumble into the black sea.

I remember how afterward I kept telling Barney about what a complete idiot I obviously was, and how worthless I had become and how much I really did hate myself.

He kept saying that he knew how I felt, and it wasn't a pretend thing that some people say when they're trying to help you. I knew more or less for certain he was telling the truth.

The truth's a fairly important thing to hold on to when you've been pulled out of the sea after wanting to drown in it. I could've let the sea take me. I could easily be dead now, which is funny when you think about it. When I say funny, what I actually mean is weird and kind of disturbing.

When there's the loud sound of a siren screaming in your head, it doesn't take too long before a feeling of not caring what happens washes over you and you become recklessly self-destructive. I used to be full of energy and happiness but I could barely remember those kinds of feelings anymore. The cheerful, childish things I used to think had been replaced. A whole load of new realizations had begun to grow inside me like tangled weeds, and they were starting to kill me. That's why I'd made the decision that involved heading off to the pier on my bike in the middle of the night and cycling off it.

The plans I'd once had had been ruined and by the time that night came, they felt like the bent-up metal of a car crash and there was nothing left—nothing that wasn't warped and destroyed, nothing that made any sense.

I didn't manage to kill myself. And when I discovered I couldn't even do that properly, I decided to do the next best thing. I decided to stay away, and to pretend I'd died. For a while, afterward, part of me wanted someone to come and find me.

It was a bit annoying the way nobody seemed to look that hard. Within a distressingly short space of time, everyone seemed to be fairly happy to assume I was a goner—after a search that can only be described as halfhearted—and get back to their lives as quickly as possible. A couple of policemen did call at Barney's house, but as soon as he told them to go away and stop bothering him, that's what they did.

You shouldn't give up on people when they vanish. You shouldn't go, "What a terrible pity but, oh well, that's that."

In actual fact, the disappearance of someone is exactly

everyone's cue to get out and search, and keep searching and not stop until there's dirt under their fingernails and wretchedness in their souls from the number of rocks they have pushed aside to see whether I'm under one of them. If you want to know my opinion, coming to terms with someone's disappearance is a bit of an offense. It's an insult to someone's memory.

I learned a lot, though. As the days passed, I learned that staying lost made its own sort of sense. I learned that there's not that much difference between pretending to be dead and really being dead. As far as I can see, both seem to amount to the same thing.

I learned that if someone you know disappears you shouldn't automatically jump to conclusions. You should ask questions, and look, and search until you know for sure. Don't write them off until you've exhausted every avenue. Keep hope in your heart.

# the third slice

According to the reports, Oscar had taken his old mountain bike from his garage and he'd gone rattling off along the road over Hallow Bridge, whose lights always look as though they're winking at you. People were saying he must have freewheeled from the top and launched himself into the sea.

"Is there any proof that he did that? Where's the evidence?" Stevie and I had asked each other when we'd met, as planned, the midnight after Oscar's mass.

"There was the bike," said Stevie. "They did find his bike. One of the divers fished it out, twisted and dripping. Someone propped it up against the last stone bollard over there and it stayed like that for a few days."

Stevie trundled over to the bollard and circled it slowly.

"Nobody wanted to touch it or move it. It was like a curse everyone was a bit afraid of. People wouldn't even *look* at it. You could see them carefully making sure they kept their eyes away from it."

Stevie said he'd looked at it, though—he didn't have a problem with it. You have to examine all the clues very carefully if you're going to get to the bottom of something. He said he'd kept coming back to look at it a load of times, until his dad had organized for someone to take the bike away. He said there had been something a bit human about the way it leaned over, as if it was looking for comfort from the cold bollard.

Loads of other people had visited the pier in the days after Oscar had gone—to leave flowers and to shake their heads at one another, but mainly, Stevie said, to be snoopy and nosy.

Mrs. Gilhooly from up the road—always a major drama queen, even at the best of times—had been an expert, my dad had said, in stirring up commotion. She'd sighed as she'd busied herself around the pier, talking to the scuba divers and filling people in on the latest developments.

"How cruel! The way that bollard stands hard and solid and insensitive, just as it must have done when that poor boy flung himself in."

Stevie said he'd got really angry with Mrs. Gilhooly, and he'd started telling her she shouldn't make comments about things she knew nothing about.

"How do you know he flung himself in? Why are you jumping to that conclusion? If my brother is supposed to be so dead, then where," he'd demanded, "where is his body? Tell me that if you're so sure!"

And nosy Mrs. Gilhooly had asked Stevie where his father was because it didn't do for grieving little boys in wheelchairs to be hanging around on their own at the site of their brother's tragic demise, in what seemed to her like a vulnerable and out-of-control condition.

Stevie had told her that for her information, he wasn't grieving. He was looking and searching and thinking very hard—and other important stuff that nobody else was doing properly. He had informed her that he was allowed to do anything he liked and that what he did, or where he went—on his own, or with anyone else—was nobody's business, especially not hers.

I hated the thought of that prying woman upsetting Stevie.

But I had to ask him some tough questions myself, even if they were difficult to think about.

"Might he have been that unhappy, Stevie? Do you think something could have happened to make him want to, you know, do something like that?"

"Look, everyone gets a bit sad once in a while. Doesn't make them suicidal."

"Yeah, I know, but maybe . . ."

"Meg," he said, holding up his hand like a little shield, "I need to be able to rely on you to keep the faith. You have to believe that he's alive. If we stop believing that, then nobody will be rooting for him, and wherever he is right now, he needs someone on his side. Don't you see? It's obvious he's just gone somewhere for a while. I know he's coming back. Our job is to find out where that somewhere is, and do whatever we need to do to help him come home. This is not the time for any doubt, Meg. It's really important. In fact, it is the most important thing we'll ever have to believe in our whole lives."

I said okay, but I knew he'd spotted the hesitation in me.

Pessimism is a contagious feeling, and there was a lot of it around. Part of me had kind of begun to imagine Oscar doing the thing everyone said he had done, and I'm not exactly sure why, but I'd even started to hear a watery kind of splashing noise before I fell asleep, and I'd begun to dream that I could see Oscar's body floating somewhere, with the black water slapping, slow and salty against his pale, dead, shoeless body.

Hundreds of people had been involved in the search. Stevie had told me that he and his dad had been at the pier when a scuba diver found Oscar's shoes. The diver had handed them to his dad, and his dad had put them carefully into his backpack and you could see wet patches spreading out as he walked off toward his car. Stevie said it was as if that bag had suddenly become the map of an unknown continent full of huge, dark, uneven-looking countries.

Stevie kept on claiming that no one was trying hard enough, but from what I could see, lots of people were doing everything they could. For a long time whole teams of guys in flippers and wet suits flapped around on the pier during the day taking big, exaggerated steps before plunging in to look for more evidence, or piling into orange boats and heading farther out over the water.

People didn't call it the search for Oscar's body, but gradually everyone knew that's what it was. Again and again they dived along that whole rocky coast.

And then, as hope of finding Oscar was gradually fading, his dad kept on trampling along the craggiest parts of the shore with binoculars pretty much permanently stuck to his face.

It wasn't logical, that's what a lot of people said, but his dad must have kept on believing, like Stevie did, like I was trying to—otherwise what was he doing out in all weathers, searching, searching, searching?

"Hey, Meggy," he would say whenever we bumped into each other, and he'd smile. But it wasn't a proper smile. It looked more like some heavy thing was being pulled across his face.

"Hey, Mr. Dunleavy," I would say back to him and he'd tell me to call him Bill.

"How's Stevie?"

It was one of those questions you ask so as to have something to say. I already knew how Stevie was.

Stevie's bedroom was downstairs in the Dunleavy house, on account of the wheelchair. If I'd been in my own house, I'd have been able to talk to him from our living room, just like I'd done from my bedroom upstairs with Oscar. But I wasn't in my own house. The Killealys—Paloma and her mother—were in it. I'd started cycling over there as often as I could, and hanging around outside his window, right beside the squashed-up cherry tree underneath the space that once belonged to me and Oscar.

Sometimes we'd look up and see Paloma's light going on but we didn't say anything about her. I didn't care if she thought I was some kind of prowler. I didn't even want to think about her, though all the time it felt as if she was very close.

"Stevie's fine, thanks, Meggie," said Bill Dunleavy. "To be honest with you, he's a lot more cheerful than you might expect. The heartbreaking thing is he keeps telling me that Oscar's absolutely excellent, that he's in a safe place, doing really well. Honestly, Meg, it would be almost funny, if the whole thing wasn't so desperately sad."

He laughed a strange kind of a laugh and pulled the back of his hand across his eyes and sniffed a bit.

"I'm trying my best, Meg. I'm trying to stay focused on Stevie because you have to give your energy to the living—it's what everyone keeps telling me. In fact, Stevie's the one who spends most of his time reassuring me: 'I'm fine Dad,' he says. 'I'm really okay. You don't have to worry.'"

It was as if Oscar's dad had forgotten that he was talking to anyone at all, and he began to mutter things then that I wasn't able to hear. His big shoulders slumped, his binoculars dangled sadly, twirling a little despondent, demented pirouette at the end of their string.

Part of me felt like telling him to stop his obsessive searching and go home. Stevie could probably have benefited from his only remaining parent being present these days. But another part of me thought that if Oscar's dad stopped looking, it would be the final turning point of despair, and I wasn't ready for that.

As the early days of the search grew into weeks, you could see that the frantic activity stopped being quite so frantic and people began to shake their heads slightly as they walked away from their daily search, and the panic that had been in everyone's voices in the early days, well, it started to fade. Panic might feel like a bad thing, but in actual fact, it contains thousands of little splinters of hope. When panic is gone, it usually means that those splinters are gone too. Even Oscar's dad looked as if he had given up, and he had started to talk about Oscar as though he was definitely dead.

And so, everyone came to accept the unacceptable. Oscar wasn't coming back. He hadn't left any of himself behind, unless you count the bike. And the waterlogged shoes.

The whole time I kept wishing I'd never gone away on that stupid trip to New Zealand, because I was sure that if I hadn't, Oscar would be here and I wouldn't be staring into the dark wondering what the bloody hell had happened, and how things had got so bad that he'd come to make such a terrible, hope-deprived decision.

It had been practically a whole year before all this that my parents had first mentioned the trip. I'd thought it was a mad idea that they would talk about for a few days and then forget. But quite quickly, their enthusiasm for leaving home got more intense and more detailed and soon they were talking about nothing else. They seemed entirely amazed that I wasn't doing the same.

Things started appearing in our house, like huge posters of surfers and dolphins and sheep and sunshine. With massive fanfare, my mother stuck them to the wall of the den, *removing* pictures of mine which, as far as I was concerned, was a perfect metaphor for the way in which this whole New Zealand plan was barging into my life and overwriting the plan I had myself—the one that involved staying where I was.

Life is hard enough when you're fourteen. You don't want to stack the odds even further against you by moving away from everything that's even vaguely familiar to you and being forced to start over again in a completely different place.

But before I knew it the tickets were booked, the plans were made and Dad was hogging the iPad so that he could Skype his brilliant new colleagues on the other side of the world.

Mum started folding our belongings into huge plastic boxes with lids on them. And they put an ad in the local paper telling the world that our house was available to rent for the six months that we were going to be away.

And then there was only a week left, and I was beginning to realize things that I'd never realized before.

I had to pack too—the things I was supposed to take with me, and the things I was supposed to leave behind. It felt wrong, stuffing my favorite hoodies and boots and tracksuit bottoms away when I should have been pulling them out.

There'd been a few fairly massive fights in my house before we left. Oscar had claimed he'd been able to hear every word due to my mother's habit of throwing the windows wide open as soon as it was June. He reckoned that I'd sounded mean and ungrateful, which according to him was in no way consistent with my real personality. He said he hardly recognized the new angry me. I was a strange girl sometimes, he said, difficult to figure out.

Our houses were so close together that me and Oscar could talk to each other from our bedroom windows. I remember the exact moment he came to the neighborhood. We were both kids then. The removal van had darkened our kitchen as it passed by and I'd peered over from the front door, and that's when I'd seen him, tall even then, and thoughtful and faraway-looking. I remember the first time I saw Stevie too, small and chatty in his wheelchair, and their dad, carefully taking out these gigantic boxes and stacking them in the front garden, but not saying a word and with no expression of expectation that you might imagine there would be on the face of someone who's moving into a new home.

Later I'd spotted Oscar again, this time from my bedroom, sitting in his window, staring at the sky, the breeze in his face, his chin resting on his arms. A gigantic telescope was right beside him, which, from time to time, he peered into. In the beginning, I'd pretended not to see him; I don't really know why. Then from the cherry tree that was squashed between our houses, he'd broken off a dead branch and whacked it on my window. When I opened it, he said "hi" and stood there smiling at me.

Oscar had a straightforward, dimpled, happy smile. It was one of the hundreds of great things about him.

And after that we were best friends. It had been as simple and inevitable as the striking of a match.


He came over all the time and we'd hang out. One day we sat under the kitchen table in my house and carved our names on it where nobody could see. And from then on that table was special because it had our secret underneath.

You don't notice yourself growing up, but one day, sooner or later, it's just not comfortable to sit under the kitchen table anymore. When we were old enough to be allowed out on our own, the first place we used to go was the harbor to throw stones into the water. We took it in turns to see who could skim theirs farthest. I always used to win, but he didn't care.

"Everyone has their special skills," he'd say, "and one of yours happens to be a strong intuitive sense of the aerodynamics and contact requirements of disc-shaped seashore skimming stones."

He'd make me laugh almost all the time with the way he spoke, and the things he said.

We got to sitting at our windows, late at night, at the end of every day. He was different from anyone I'd ever met, and when Oscar was my friend, nothing was annoying or complicated. Everything was simple and enjoyable and fun. Everything made sense.

I don't remember now who took the photo of us, but I've had it in my room for years. We're leaning out of our windows and we're laughing at each other with a joyfulness purer than anything to do with the polite smiling you get used to doing when you get older. That photo has the kind of proper smiles that happen when you're looking straight into the face of someone who's been your best friend for a long time.

During the weeks before the trip, our talks had taken on a new and mournful tone. I'd sit at my window sniffing while Oscar sat at his, looking at me with a tender kind of a frown on his face. He had this way of swinging his legs from side to side with his hands on the window frame, holding on. I'd developed a habit myself that involved picking the loose plaster off our outside wall. It was a measly kind of rebellion—my resentful response to feeling so sorrowful and so misunderstood.

The nights before I left were hotter than I had ever remembered. But in our town, even on the stillest of summer nights, the cold is never far away.

I told him about how I didn't want to go—how my parents were robbing me of my most fundamental human right by making me do something that was completely against my will. I told him about what nightmares I was having because of the gigantically hard job it was going to be to get to know bunches of New Zealand people I'd never met, and who already had friends and weren't in the market for a new pale red-haired freckly one from Ireland.

Even though Oscar Dunleavy was my friend, it didn't mean he automatically agreed with everything I said, or believed the things I believed. And when it came to the trip, he was definitely on my parents' side. He told me I should embrace it, which is exactly what Mum and Dad had been saying the whole time too. Embracing it, he reckoned, was the only way anyone should treat an opportunity like the one that was being handed to me on a plate.

"It's really not something to complain about," he had said, pointing out that I was going somewhere brilliant and different for half a year, and reminding me that I'd be living in a house that had a swimming pool in the garden and a fantastic lake nearby surrounded by mountains. He said that if I was grumpy about a trip like that, people would get jealous of me—they'd think I was taking for granted something that hardly anyone ever got a chance to do, which is to get away from the life they're living, and try a completely new one for a while.

According to him, it could be quite bad luck to have the evil eye of resentment following me around when I was in the middle of getting used to a whole different country.

I tried to explain to Oscar how dangerous and unrelenting the sun was going to be and how, compared to the New Zealand people, I would look so pale that everyone was going to assume I had some serious illness or pigmentation-related disability. I was sure to be marked out as a misfit, and I was positive that no one was going to talk to me.

"They're going to be *dying* to talk to you," he had said. "Nobody's going to think there's anything wrong with you. You'll be so exotic and fascinating and pretty much the whole population will want to be your friend. Plus, there are things that have been invented for hot climates, you know, like sunblock. Air-conditioning. T-shirts. Meg, there's a solution to every problem. What you're doing right now is looking for reasons not to want to go."

He told me that within a few short weeks I'd have forgotten all my unwillingness about the trip and that I'd be populating my Facebook page with photos of smiling sunny fantasticness.

Meanwhile, back here, he reminded me, the Irish winter would be sneaking up on everyone. The mornings would be growing colder and gloomier, and getting up for school would be the depressing activity that we both knew well. By the time October came everyone's teeth would be chattering, their hands fused in clawlike grips around the handlebars of their bikes because of the icy rain that would be pelting down from a great height.

"How many people do you know who have ever had the chance of a sunshine-filled expedition to a new bright land with white beaches and outdoor parties and surfing lessons?"

I kept doing my best to try to think that he was right. But there was an anger in me that seeped into almost everything during those weeks before I left. My parents hadn't had the decency to check with me, not even out of curiosity, whether the trip was something I was interested in. I couldn't stop thinking about that, and dwelling on it, and it had soured the air around me.

I'd wanted a mature discussion, which would have included me informing my parents—because it had obviously escaped their notice—that I wasn't cut out for New Zealand, what with my love of temperate climates and my shrimplike complexion.

Oscar said lots of things to me from his window in those weeks before I left. He told me that he'd miss me a lot. He told me that he had a whole load of information about New Zealand, which was going to come in fairly handy. He said he'd email it to me as soon as I arrived.

I wanted to say lots of things to him too. Things that had gradually become clearer just before I was supposed to leave. But sometimes the things you want to say most are exactly the things that somehow you are least able to.

And then there were the things my parents kept *on* saying such as, "Meg, thousands of children would be so *grateful* for an opportunity like this." And, "We really have no idea why you're being so difficult."

I went over to Oscar and Stevie and their dad and they all said things wouldn't be the same without me, and Stevie whizzed in circles. He said he was making a force field that would stop me from being able to leave, but his dad told him he was making everyone dizzy.

When you're supposed to feel positive and warm about something that's filling you with a rigid kind of dread, it makes you quiet. It makes you not want to talk to people. It makes you wish you could tell everyone to go away and leave you alone.

My parents had started to beg.

"Please, Meg," they would say as I flopped on the sofa in a listless stupor that can only happen when you're feeling as sad and uncertain as I was.

"Will you please do your best not to be so sullen and gloomy."

Gradually they gave up, the way logical people do when begging is not making any difference. Instead they became sullen and gloomy themselves. They began to speak about the trip as if it was going to be an unavoidable ordeal. They'd lost the excitement that they'd started out with. They talked about the travel arrangements in whispers as if they were sharing news of a sudden illness or some massively expensive bill they hadn't been expecting. Soon it was as if some big sword was swinging over their heads.

I felt guilty. I'd infected the house with a crotchety mood. My parents' prospect of their trip of a lifetime had been drained of its happiness and it was my fault.

The whole world felt bar-taut and joyless. And it probably would have stayed like that. That's if it hadn't been for Oscar.

Me and Oscar never used to get bored talking to each other at the windows. When we'd been younger we'd got into the habit of telling each other lots of quite personal things. Our best subjects. Our favorite colors. What we wanted to be when we grew up (me: a train driver, him: a trampoline man). I never asked him what exactly a trampoline man was. I should have, but I never did. There are lots of things I should have asked him.

I couldn't stop thinking about us when we were kids, and remembering us sitting there, crouched and furtive, with our chins on our elbows talking for hours about the important stuff that little kids have to talk about, like whether it was going to snow, or what we were getting for Christmas, or when was the next time we were going to the zoo.

In the beginning, our parents had told us we weren't allowed to hang out of our windows on account of them thinking that hanging out of windows was extremely dangerous. Often they shouted for us to get back inside and say good night and go to bed. But after a while, they gave up worrying about it. It became the thing we always did. We never fell out. They bought us phones when we were eleven, saying "now you can talk to each other whenever you want." They thought we'd be thrilled, but we weren't. We were horrified. We didn't need phones as long as we lived next door to each other. Oscar kept the same old branch from that cherry tree in his room, refusing to let anyone take it away, and every night, I'd wait for his scratchy whack on my window. It was the best sound ever.

Another thing about Oscar is that he wasn't afraid of anyone. And he always made up his own mind, no matter what other people said. They're two of the best things I remember about him now.

He wasn't just my friend. He was kind of magic. I can't really explain it better than that. He was honest and he was decent and he was always cheerful. And even though his brother, Stevie, had to use a wheelchair, it wasn't a problem the way people usually think it is, because Oscar always made sure that every door was opened and every stairway had a ramp, and every train station had the right access so he could get in. He used to say that if the world was designed properly, the whole population would be flying around the place in wheelchairs. And when he said that, Stevie used to laugh.

Oscar's hobby was saving people. He used to save people all the time, and fix things that were broken and catch people when they were falling. It wasn't a skill that you'd immediately know about or notice. Stevie said that Oscar had a gift and the gift was that he could *smell* things that you wouldn't imagine would smell of anything—things like sadness and desperation. Things like fear and hopelessness.

He never made a big deal about it, but he was quiet and confident—and when you believe in your own abilities, you are much more likely to be always ready to act on them, which Oscar always was. Whenever I asked him about it, he claimed that his were not exceptional or extraordinary abilities in the slightest. Everyone, he said, is able to tell when someone is in need of help, but few people really take the time to listen to their instincts, and that, he said, was the only difference between him and a lot of other people.

It wasn't the only thing about him that was different. Oscar used to make apple tarts. I never thought there was anything remarkable about them until one night, a while before I left.

I think of it still, even when I'm trying not to.

# the fourth slice

When you live on the coast, you get used to the thousand sounds of the sea—booming one day so that you have to cover your ears, another day smacking on the rocks like the sound of giants clapping. Sometimes crashing, sometimes rippling, other times pattering. The coast is a moody place. Each day is different. Nothing ever stays the same.

It had been a summery midnight in June. The air was warm and muffled, and the sea was quiet, but little chilly strands sneaked up from its surface, weaving in and out of the warmth as they often did around our place, even in the hottest weather.

The moon wobbled with a silver brightness so it looked as if it might be breathing, and Meg Molony sat, extremely spectacular in her window—her lovely face sprinkled with freckles, her hands picking pieces of plaster off the wall, her face peering out into the night.

I'd been busy that evening because I'd had one of my hunches.

"Have you been making apple tarts again?" she asked, frowning and smiling at the same time.

"Yes, as a matter of fact, that's exactly what I've been doing. How did you know?"

She pointed at my hair. I shook my head and the cloud of white flour that floated up made us both laugh.

I tried to explain again about my apple-tart habit. Some people can tell from the way their bones feel that there will be bad weather coming. Some people can tell where water is buried under the ground. My ability was being able to smell things in the air, heavy things full of longing. Those smells were my sign that it was time to get baking.

She said that whenever I told her about the apple-tart thing, I had a way of speaking that made it sound logical and ordinary even though it actually wasn't.

And right then, as I had expected to, I sensed it. I had to straighten up and lean farther out the window and get Meg to stop talking.

"Hang on a moment, Meg," I'd said and she'd said,

"What, Oscar, what is it?"

I had to get quiet and I took the telescope and looked off beyond our houses toward the pier. I could hear something nobody else could hear, and I saw something nobody else could see.

Meg was trying her best too, listening with me pretty intently while her white curtain flapped droopily around her, like a tired little ghost.

A minute or so had gone by.

"I think someone's there," I whispered.

Meg's eyes were wide and I could see from the way she was moving that she wanted to be in on the whole thing.

"I smell it, Meg, it's really strong now."

"I can't smell anything," she said.

"You probably can if you concentrate a bit more."

She did concentrate a bit more but it didn't make any difference.

"What does it smell of?" she asked me.

"It smells like someone in need; it's full of despair. Worse than fear—much more destructive. Down on the pier. I've got to go."

I grabbed a blanket and stuffed it into my backpack. One of my apple tarts was at the ready in a white cardboard box and I had to hold it like a waiter carrying a tray. It's a miracle how it stayed in one piece as I climbed out of the window and clambered down the tree. I'd been practicing my moves, and it had obviously started to pay off.

"Ouch," I said a few times before landing on the ground. I had to hop around for a bit, rubbing my elbow and still balancing the tart while Meg asked me if I was okay. I told her I was totally fine.

My bike was glinting at the gate.

"A man is there, Meggy. He's at the edge of the sea. Somebody's got to save him before it's too late."

"A man? On his own? By the edge of the sea, at midnight? How has that got anything to do with you?"

I'm not really sure why, but I never worried whether something was my business or not.

Meg said that it was really great being my best friend. But she also said it was exhausting.

"Are you seriously going to go? Now? At this time of night?"

"Meg, didn't you hear me? Someone's in need of help."

"How do you know? Maybe he's fine. Is it even slightly possible that whoever he is, he wants to be on his own?"

"Yeah. Possible. But my instincts tell me not."

"Can I come with you then?"

"You can if you like," I said, "but keep in mind that time may be running out."

It turns out I was right. It was a man. Down at the end, gazing into the sparkly blackness right next to the rusty, barnacled ladder that scaled the deep side of the pier.

He seemed very old. A scraggy little dog trotted nervously up and down, looking at the water, then looking back at the man, and then looking at the water again. Stashed by the wall there was a slumped-looking blanket, full of holes, and two sad, crumpled bags huddled together like frightened people. The man was a maze of wrinkles and his hands were dirty. Tears made shiny branchlike patterns on his cheeks.

In the gentlest voice I could find, I asked him what he was doing.

"Oh dear me," he said. "Would you take my dog, please." He didn't look at us. He kept staring into the water as if there was something there that he had lost.

"I left Homer safe, away from the sea," he continued, "and I've written to the RSPCA and he was going to be absolutely fine, but the silly fellow followed me down here and I can't persuade him otherwise."

The dog sat uncertainly beside the man. The man's voice was flat and kind of distant and unexpectedly posh.

"That dog, goodness, but he's always had an unrivaled ability to sniff, and he's found me here and for the most part, he's a great boy—aren't you, Homer?—but you see . . . just at this minute, I'd much rather be alone."

I knelt on the knobbly granite. Homer came over to me and took a few good sniffs and he must have concluded that I was okay and that I could be trusted because he rested his chin on my knee for a few seconds before resuming his nervous trotting.

"Will I take the dog?" Meg whispered, and I knew she was doing her best to be helpful.

"No, Meggy, the dog stays," I whispered back.

And right then, I knew that the things I said to him were going to be important and so I thought for a few moments about exactly what I was going to say and then, as clearly and slowly as I could, I started to talk.

"I know what you might be thinking here on your own, but those thoughts won't last forever," I said. "You won't always feel like this. This will pass. Homer will be here for you, and the sun will rise and you'll find your reasons again, the ones you think have deserted you. Isn't that right, Meg?" I said, turning to her as hints of a new summer morning started to rustle and stir and birds began to sing.

The man told us his name was Barney. Barney Brittle. He put his head in his hands and spoke in this low, exhausted voice: "Children, you're both very kind, but please take my dog and leave me. I would much rather you went back to your homes, thank you. This does not concern you. I would like to be left in peace." Nobody moved for what felt like a long time.

I knew it was time. I delved into my bag and pulled out the box made of white card, and I had to lift it quite delicately, because apple tarts are fragile and this one was important. I presented it to Barney.

"Here," I said, "I made this for you."

Barney lifted his head and looked at me holding out the box to him.

"How on earth could you have made something for me? You've only just met me."

His eyes shone suddenly with something brighter and more curious than you might have expected to see right then in the face of that old man.

He took a slice and held it up to his face and he closed his eyes and breathed in deeply.

"I must admit," he said, "that does smell rather good."

"Rather good?" I'd scolded him, putting on a fake offended voice and trying to lighten the atmosphere a bit. "Em, I think you'll find that it's a bit better than rather good."

"Oh will I now?" said Barney, but you could see that he was warming to the apple tart, and to us.

He took a bite. And he closed his eyes and after another minute or two he said, "That, my goodness, that is quite something."

"See," I said, and I started to feel relieved, and proud and happy.

"Oh my gosh," said Barney, "did you really make this yourself? I haven't tasted anything like that since, since . . . I've never tasted anything like this before. This is . . . why it's *sublime.*"

"I know," I said.

Homer's mood had totally changed and he was beside himself with the kind of delight that dogs communicate by shaking their entire bodies and rushing in and out between people's legs.

Meg and I had a slice too, and we even gave a little to Homer. We sat munching and smiling and there was that comfortable feeling that sometimes happens when there's no need for conversation.

A wild splash of sunshine poured across the sea from the island and everything was flooded by a golden glow. I looked at my phone. We'd been there for hours longer than it had seemed. I'd be completely murdered if my dad found out that I was out of bed, not to mention out of the house, at the pier, talking to strangers and eating tart.

"You take the rest home with you," I said to Barney, "—it's yours."

"Oh dear boy, thank you very much indeed. I do think I shall be off. And I suggest the time is long gone for you two to get back under your covers. I feel I've done quite enough in keeping you awake in these small hours."

We shook hands and smiled at each other.

"You're going to be okay," I said to him and he said, "Yes, yes, in point of fact, I daresay I will."

And Meg and I grabbed our bikes and we both headed up the lane.

I made her wear my shoes on the way back, which were too big for her.

"Oscar, has anyone ever told you how strange you are?"

"Yes. You. Practically every day."

"Well, that's because you are."

"Makes me more lovable, doesn't it? Admit it," I said, and I pushed her gently with my shoulder and she said, "Yeah right, sure thing."

We went back to our houses and we waved to each other from our rooms.

"What am I going to do without you, Oscar?"

"You'll be fine," I answered. "You could probably do with some time away from me. I'm a pain in the neck. You're always saying so."

"You're right," she said. "It'll be great to have you out of my hair for a few months... Oscar, seriously though."

"What?"

"Stay in touch, will you? Please?"

"Of course I will."

"Promise?"

"Yes, I promise."

"Good, because I'm really going to miss you."

# the fifth slice

It was hard to keep up with Oscar. Take that night we first met Barney. One minute Oscar was sitting at the window, swinging his legs as usual, and the next minute he was flinging himself out of the window and doing these trapeze-artist moves down the cherry tree, armed with an apple tart. And then he was gone, a silver streak in the night, his feet a blurry circle.

Oh bloody hell, I'd thought, as I'd got my own hoodie on, pulled the window to its fully open position and launched myself at the tree, as Oscar had done. And like Oscar, I'd practically fallen out of it, except that the branches had helpfully broken my fall. I'd scrambled to my feet and tiptoed toward the garage, whose door had creaked agonizingly loudly as I'd opened it to grab my own bike, hoping that my parents weren't going to wake up.

"Oscar," I had said under my breath. I could see him, by now far off, a flash of light bobbing slightly in the distance like he was floating on a choppy sea.

"Oscar, Oscar, Oscar," I whispered again, heading as fast as I could in the direction of the pier. That's something I've got used to doing, whispering his name under my breath in my head like that, over and over again.

"This is an apple tart," Oscar had said solemnly to Barney that night as if it was the answer to everything, and as if it contained a million explanations of its own.

"But it's not an ordinary apple tart. It's the apple tart of hope. After you've taken a bite, the whole world will look almost completely different. Things will start to change and by the time you've had a whole slice you'll realize that everything is going to be okay. "

And when Barney took a bite, his face did change. I'm not claiming there was anything magic about his tarts but I will say they tasted great.

"You keep an eye on the dog," Oscar whispered to me, "and I'll have a bit more of a chat with Barney." I called the dog over to me and sat patting him while Oscar and Barney talked for a while and though I couldn't hear everything they said, after a while, I could hear them laughing. Oscar's chuckle echoed toward me and then off over the sea, followed by the old man's low, wheezy guffaw, which sounded something like relief or liberty. At least it was a surprisingly cheery kind of a sound, which made me feel something that I could not precisely name—something comforting I guess. A nice warm kind of a thing, which was handy as well as nice, considering how I was standing in my bare feet, wondering why I was there at all, with the ends of my PJ bottoms feeling muddy and damp.

"No offense, but I didn't expect him to have such a nice voice," I'd said after we'd said good-bye to Barney and were heading home.

"Perhaps that's because you haven't spoken to many people like him before."

I'd never even *met* anyone like Barney before.

It was like that when I hung out with Oscar—always doing something new. Thinking in a fresh way. Meeting someone different.

Oscar had acted as if his apple-tart strategy was the most normal, unremarkable thing ever. He didn't seem to realize that he was out of the ordinary. If anyone else in the entire world *had* thought of baking an apple tart from scratch, and if by the same miracle they saved another human being in the way that Oscar just had, they would probably look triumphant or at least a bit smug or self-satisfied. But Oscar had the same plain look on his face.

And lying in my bed that night, I thought about the trip to New Zealand, and how near it was getting, and how excited I should be feeling, and I asked myself why I so desperately didn't want to go.

The truth tumbled on top of me right then like a marshmallowy sackful of soft sweet simple things. The feeling was colorful and clear and gentle and full of certainty and it pummeled me gently inside and out, and I understood. I understood these battles I'd been having with my parents and why an adventure away from Oscar felt like such a terrible thing.

I didn't want to leave him. I didn't want to sit by a new window in a strange house in a foreign country and not be able to talk to him. Oscar was the reason. He was the reason I wanted to stay.

Our departure date got even closer, of course, and then because you can't hold things back, it arrived. It was very early and I was still in bed, hoping for some disaster to happen that would mean we didn't have to go, when Oscar's familiar tap, tap, tapping came at the window.

I rolled out of bed with a thump and hobbled over to the window, getting ready to say the good-bye that I didn't want to say. Oscar wasn't there. Instead, a patchy smudge of condensation was on the window as if someone had breathed on it, and when I pulled the window open the first thing I felt was a tiny familiar gust of cinnamony sweet-smelling warm air rising into my face. A rope and two pulleys had been constructed between our houses.

And swinging slightly on a little suspended shelf—in a box made of the same white cardboard I'd seen him carry to the pier that night—sat one of Oscar's apple tarts. It had a golden baked letter M right in the middle and a tiny pastry airplane with pastry clouds around it and a little pastry smiley face. And a particular smell surrounded me, the one you get when butter and sugar and spices have been mingled into a single thing and cooked in a hot oven.

I could hear my mum storming up and down stairs. I could hear my dad's voice, tense and grouchy. The phone kept ringing and my parents kept roaring at each other to answer it. The air fizzed with a kind of prickly energy that happens when people have been bombarded with a relentless campaign of resistance and are now filled with uncertainty about a big decision they've made that's too late to back out of.

I pulled the tart indoors from its little swinging shelf, took it downstairs and put it on the kitchen table.

"Where did that come from?" Mum asked, stopping suddenly and gazing at the golden raised pastry.

"Oscar," I said as if that explained everything. When my dad saw the M and the clouds and the airplane and the smiley face, he smiled too.

And in a series of enchanted slow-motion movements, the three of us got ready to eat the tart. My dad lifted three plates out of the cupboard, I put the kettle on for tea and my mum rummaged around for a knife. Carefully, she placed a crumbly appley sweet slice in front of each of us.

A new feeling settled on the room—a feeling that didn't have any resentment or stress in it. And as the pastry melted in our mouths, other things seemed to melt too, like misgivings and doubts and the things that had made us grumpy and withdrawn.

The shadows of our uncertainty seemed to disappear.

I know that possibly sounds a bit peculiar, but after each of us had taken a few bites, all of a sudden, everything looked different.

Something good and open-minded started waking up inside my head, and I surprised even myself by making a short speech about how much I admired my parents' adventurous spirits and how I was determined to make this a worthwhile trip for all of us and how I was going to try to be much nicer about the whole plan.

Mum and Dad had looked at each other and then turned to me and said how good this was of me and how mature and how decent. And then both of them gave me a warm sweet apple-tart hug.

"I mean honestly," Mum said later. "Is there a single other teenager you know in the world who'd go to such elaborate lengths to make and deliver something like that—who'd notice how busy and stressed we have been and how it's been quite a while since we've had anything homemade? So exquisitely baked! He must have made that pastry himself. That's very unusual indeed. And such thoughtful, appropriate, carefully cut out motifs on the top! There's really no one like him."

"No," I said, "there isn't."

After that, getting ready to leave stopped feeling like a big negative chore and began to feel more like a celebration.

"Be sure to say thank you to Oscar for that tart," my mum had said, looking kind of mystified and happy, while Dad had nodded dreamily in the background.

"Okay, I will," I said.

Who would've guessed that something so specific, so definite, so full of butter and sugar would have been the answer to my fears? It turns out, though, that Oscar's tart was the solution. Such a simple thing.

Oscar said that now that I was committed to the trip, it was going to be better than even he'd predicted. As soon as I arrived, everything was going to be instantly fantastic—I was going to have a wonderful time and it was all going to work out perfectly brilliantly.

But along with these new warm feelings, there was something else too. The thing that had been haunting me swelled up inside me again, and I couldn't keep it to myself any longer, which is often a time, I have found, when it is important to write something down.

*Dear Oscar,*

*I don't know how to say this any other way, but, you see, I need to explain something. I can't stop thinking about that night when you rescued Barney with your tart—and how good and kind I realize you've always been. It wasn't until this morning when you sent me an apple tart of my own that I finally knew what it is that I have to tell you.*

*The timing is pretty terrible, but, you see, the reason I haven't wanted to go away is because I've wanted to stay here, and the reason I've wanted to stay here is because of you.*

*I've nothing against New Zealand or anything but because of how I feel, specifically about you, the whole world looks different.*

*I don't know whether it's because everything has got darker or lighter. I guess that depends on how you feel about me which is, I hope, the same.*

*So anyway, look, you've convinced me that I should, as you say, "embrace the adventure" so that is what I have decided to do. It was the taste of your apple tart that finally made up my mind to give this my all. But I need to know you'll be here when I come back.*

*I love you, Oscar Dunleavy.*

*I've been falling in love with you since the day we first met.*

*I need to have some idea about whether you feel the same way about me. Send me a sign. Anything will do.*

*Love,*

*Meg*


I put my hand flat on the paper and I thought for an insane moment that I'd stroll over to his house and drop it into the mailbox. I wondered about the possible things that Oscar would say or think or do if I'd ever had the courage to send it.

I never sent the letter because I was afraid. I was afraid he would laugh at me. I was afraid that what I had written would seem ridiculously stupid. I was afraid it might break something that me and Oscar already had. I was afraid that he didn't . . . that he would never feel the same way. So even though I put the letter in an envelope, and even though I wrote "To Oscar Dunleavy" on the front of it, and even though for a while I thought about running next door, right then in the middle of that night to post it, in the end I never did.

Instead I turned and twisted that letter in my hands until it got puckered and crumpled, and then I smoothed it out again and I shoved it under my mattress—a soft, silent, stifled place that nobody can see.

# the sixth slice

When Meg left for New Zealand, I missed her all the time. I'd look over at her window and when I saw her room, blank and vacant, something inside me would twist, like a pain. I'd got so used to seeing her face that not seeing it felt wrong and miserable and kind of hopeless.

So when Paloma Killealy moved in . . . of course, she wasn't Meg and she could never replace Meg or anything . . . but I did think that maybe she would be a person I might get to know, and it turns out that she thought the same, and that was pretty good, I thought. At the time.

The Energizer was on and during the first week Paloma arrived and the day before it at school, in front of a whole load of people, including Andy and Greg, Paloma asked me if I'd take her to it.

It was obvious that she'd no clue about how The Energizer worked, because it is this event that happens a couple of times a year in a big hall with fields around it outside of town.

When you arrive, you spend the whole night shouting at your

friends just so they'll be able to hear you and you watch people like Andy and Greg kissing girls. That's all that happens. It's a bit boring to tell the truth, but everyone goes. I'm not sure why.

One thing that I do know, though, is that nobody "takes" anybody else to The Energizer. That's not the way it works. I explained that to Paloma and she said, "Oh right, I see, okay then," and she walked out of the yard, and her hair swung from side to side and Andy and Greg were like, "Oscar man, are you *crazy*? She definitely wants you, and would you *look* at her?"

They claimed that our school had never had someone as fit as her in it, in its entire history, not since it was founded, which was in 1968.

"She's *giving* herself to you on a plate. What's going on inside your little head, buddy?" asked Greg, and he caught me in one of those headlocks he and Andy always loved to do.

Paloma discovered our windows, the way Meg and I had, and it wasn't long before we started chatting. It felt weird, but Paloma was nice in her own way, and it was good to see someone in that window. Plus she hadn't a clue how things in our school worked, so it was an opportunity to explain.

"I'm sorry if I embarrassed you in front of your friends," she said, and I said it was okay.

"Everything is so different here from what I'm used to. It's taking me a while to adjust," she explained. "Where I came from before, we had school dances and boys took girls to them."

"Oh right, I see," I said, and I told her she didn't have to be sorry and it was perfectly understandable that she'd assume that it was the same here.

"I have a question for you, Oscar," she said, and she leaned out of

Meg's window and she twisted her hair around her long fingers and she opened and closed her eyes slowly and I said, "Okay, well, shoot."

"I'm curious. I mean, I'm wondering—if boys *did* take girls to The Energizer, I mean—if that *was* the way it worked, you know, I wonder *then* would you be interested in taking me?'

I saw straightaway what she was getting at. She stroked her arm and tilted her head to one side, and looked at me with her liquid shiny eyes. And she did look fairly lovely all right.

I thought then that Paloma Killealy was definitely interested in me, which was a good feeling, especially considering how much almost every boy in my class had been talking about her since she arrived. At school, people sighed when she passed by and they smelled the air that she'd walked through, and Andy and Greg had become more or less obsessed with thinking about her. They never stopped asking me questions about what it was like to be her next-door neighbor.

It could have been most flattering thing that had ever happened to me. But just because a gorgeous girl is interested in you, it doesn't mean you should change your plans.

"Paloma, it's really nice of you to ask me a question like that. I really appreciate it." But then I said that I was about to tell her something that I'd never told anyone and I got her to promise to keep it to herself. She said of course she promised, and her face was as serious and trustworthy as you can imagine a face would be.

"You see, there's this girl. Her name's Meg. She used to live in the room you're in now and when you move out she'll be back, and you see most of the time, she's all I think about. I think about what she's doing. I wonder what she's thinking. If people took other people to The Energizer, Meg is the one I'd like to take. I hope you know what I mean; I hope you understand."

"Oh right," she said, and then she repeated what I had said as if it was a difficult thing to understand: "Meg's the name of the girl you're interested in."

And I said, "Yes, that's exactly it."

"So wait," she said, "what you're actually saying is that *you're* not interested in *me*?"

"No," I said because I believe people always deserve to be told the truth, "not in that way, Paloma. But I can tell you, in case you didn't already know, that apart from me, every boy in the class is really, really interested in you, so you still have a lot of choice if you ever want to—"

"*You're* not interested in *me*?" she interrupted, saying that same thing a couple more times in exactly the same tone of voice.

After that conversation, Paloma quickly got back to being herself again. She said that Meg must be a really special person for someone like me to feel those things about her. She said Meg was lucky and I said thanks.

She even asked me for Meg's email because it would be nice, she said, for her to drop her a line and introduce herself, seeing as she was renting her house and living in her room. So I wrote Meg's email address on a torn scrap of paper and I rolled it up and tossed it over to Paloma, who caught it in her long fingers and started uncrumpling it straight away and putting the details into her phone.

"Call over to me tomorrow, okay?" she said, not looking at me and pulling across Meg's curtains. And I said that I would.

Next day when I knocked on her door, Paloma's mother showed me into the back garden. Paloma was standing by the fence with a huge fanlike bat in her hands, hitting a mattress so hard that dust was rising from it in huge clouds.

"What are you doing?" I asked.

"What . . . THWACK! . . . does . . . THWACK! . . . it look like . . . THWACK! I'm doing?" she replied, panting and scowling a bit on account of the effort that this was taking.

"It looks like you're beating up a mattress."

"I'm *airing* it," she said. "Which is obviously something that your girlfriend Meg never did because it's rancid. I've no idea how on earth she expected me to sleep on it in that condition."

"For the record, she's not my girlfriend, and also for the record that conversation was confidential."

Paloma continued with her whacking and didn't reply.

"What's wrong, Paloma?"

"Why would you think there's something wrong?"

"Oh, I don't know, it's just that you look so scary and angry."

She stopped beating the mattress and she smiled at me.

"Maybe that's because I'm not used to boys rejecting me." She laughed a high, shrill, trembly laugh that didn't sound like her. I started to say something but she held her finger up to my mouth and in this juicy kind of a voice she said, "Oscar, you don't have to say anything in response to me, I was only messing."

"Of course, I knew that," I said, but messing, I mean *that* kind of messing that Paloma was doing, seemed sort of sour. It felt like biting into a bitter fruit and finding that at the gritty center there were hundreds of tiny pips of truth.

Paloma had found a letter in Meg's room addressed to me. She dropped it into the mailbox with a note attached to it: *Oscar!! Found this letter to you. I didn't read it or anything—just passing it along!! See u soon!!!!!! PalomaK xxx*

That was nice of her, I thought, looking at the envelope, which was a bit battered, and noticing that the lip of it seemed to have been opened and closed a few times because it was crushed and a little bit torn, as if Meg had possibly changed her mind and taken the letter out once or twice and then put it back in again.

I took it up to my room so I could open it in private, and before I did, I glanced across at Paloma's window. There was a new kind of light in there, strong and dazzling, making it very hard to see properly. It felt as if I'd been staring at the sun.

# the seventh slice

When you move somewhere new, the difference and adventure and surprising experience feels like its own kind of forever. The mundane, repetitive times in your life are the ones that slip away in your memory as if they've hardly happened. You'd think it would be the opposite—that the uninteresting bits would seem to take ages, and the fun times would fly by, but that's not actually the way it works.

From the moment we arrived, practically everything was sprinkled with newness and surprise—a fresh adventure around every sunny corner.

I learned to water-ski and to swim in that new strong way that you need to learn when you're swimming in a lake. Lake swimming is a silky, slippy kind of feeling. There's none of that saltiness to hold you up, so you have to work much, much harder to stay afloat. When you compare it to swimming in the Irish Sea, it is about as completely different an activity as you can get.

I got used to the hot weather and I got to know a lot of people too. And by the time January came, I'd got used to cycling to the lake for a swim almost every day after school with a bunch of my new Kiwi friends.

In Ireland, taking a swim anywhere outdoors in the middle of January is a borderline lunatic type of activity. In New Zealand it's more like a basic human right.

Houses in Rotarua are made of wood. At night they creak and groan as if they are alive. The swans on nearby Rotoiti Lake don't have the glaring blue white feathers of normal swans. They're black and sleek, and their beaks are blood red. In New Zealand, the ground underneath your feet behaves in a way you think you'll never get used to: it shudders, and most of the time no one else seems to notice, and sometimes it boils and burbles and occasionally it even spurts out hot muddy water straight up into the air.

When you're from a rainy, wet, cool, cloudy place, you're not familiar with the feeling of being blasted in the face every time you go outside, as if you were opening the door of an oven.

In the end, though, I learned to like these strange things and to cherish the differences and to appreciate the adventure. I had a brilliant time, just like Oscar had said I would.

He was right, in the way Oscar had been right about so many things. The trip did work out perfectly okay. I mean at least at first. Everything he predicted was pretty much what happened. When I felt the feelings about him creep to the surface of my brain in the way they kept on doing, I'd try to picture my mattress at home in Ireland and in my head I'd push those thoughts and feelings under it, like the letter I'd written. And then I would keep on hurling myself into New Zealand life with the careless enthusiasm of someone courageous, leaping into an unknown sea.

Mum and Dad continued to be surprised and happy by my change of heart—"thrilled" is what they said—about how much of an effort I was making.

They said my positive thinking had made all the difference.

I've discovered that you can have a great time somewhere while at the same time missing somewhere else, and I missed Ireland. I obviously missed Oscar more than you might imagine was possible for anyone to miss another human being without getting sick or permanently sad.

I used to dream about him, and in my dreams he'd always be framed by his window, swinging his legs and smiling his beautiful smile.

I'd got him to promise to tell me the minute someone even looked like they were going to move into my house. I told him that even if someone didn't move in, still he was to stay in touch on a regular basis. And he promised he would, and I did too. And so—in the beginning—we did.

To: Meg Molony
From: Oscar Dunleavy
Subject: A few things to keep in mind

Didn't want to tell you this before you left, but now that you've embraced the adventure, here are a few useful things you should probably know:

Fact number one: New Zealand harbors deeply unpleasant, often life-threatening waterborne diseases, many of which are rife throughout the country. Do not drink the water.

Fact number two: New Zealanders are a reckless people, their most popular sports including white-water rafting, bungee jumping, cricket and other generally hazardous activities. Again, avoid.

Fact number three: the weather in New Zealand can be unpredictable, so ideally do not attempt to engage in travel of any kind and stay indoors as much as possible. If you are forced to embark on a journey, never leave without a bunch of stuff including drinks, sunscreen, food, provisions, warm clothes, phone and preferably signal flares.

Fact number four: they practically have an earthquake a minute, so it is imperative that you learn the protocol for effective earthquake survival.

To: Oscar Dunleavy
From: Meg Molony

Since when have you been a health and safety expert?
M Xox

To: Meg Molony
From: Oscar Dunleavy
Meggy, take this seriously, I mean it, you can't be too careful. O xx

And then one day not long after that I saw this message from him on Facebook:

Oh hey, Meg! Sending this from my bedroom and I've seen a light in your bedroom flicker on!

I can see someone with long hair strolling around your room and slowly taking things out of her bags and hanging them up and putting stuff into drawers. Weird that it's not you, Meggy. Wish it was.

Xxx

"I know, totally," I'd replied, trying to ignore a big judder I suddenly felt inside my body.

Later he'd sent more details:

> Thought you'd like to be kept up to speed about
> the renters. You'll be delighted to hear that they are fine
> and they'll take good care of your house. Yes, that girl I
> mentioned is living in your room now but don't worry, she's
> super nice, plus tidy. It's good to have someone next door
> again. I mean obviously I'd prefer if it was you.
> Her name's Paloma. Paloma Killealy.

I don't know why, but I told him to take a photo of her and send it to me.

> Will send you a proper one when I get close up enough.
> For now you'll have to make do with this. Hope you're
> applying the sunblock and staying away from the scorpions.
> Oscar xx

I clicked on the attachment and found a picture of a person in shadow, just an outline really was all I could see, standing behind my white curtain. The person's head was bent and it looked like she was carrying some kind of unreliable light—a candle say, or a bad flashlight, and it cast strange shapes in my old bedroom making it look like a foreign place, and I wished immediately that I hadn't asked Oscar to take any photograph at all, or now that he had, I wished that he hadn't sent it to me.

Not long after that, he sent another photo just as he had promised. It wasn't any clearer, with a dark shadow still covering her face, but it was of her sitting on my window ledge, with her body leaning forward in a way that it only would be if you knew the person who was taking the photo extremely well.

After a while, Oscar didn't really talk much about anything or anyone else.

He seemed to have learned a huge number of details about her, like she was coming to our school, and how she had a mother who was a businesswoman and how they were looking for a bigger house while they rented ours and how she didn't like certain things in my house: for example it was much too small and the pipes rattled whenever you turned the faucets on, and how the boiler room had a funny smell and how the shower beside her room was totally unpredictable—scalding one moment and freezing to death the next.

"Tell her they're not unpredictable," I wrote back to Oscar. "Tell her that she only has to get to know them properly."

He said he'd pass that along, and then he went on about how she had massive brown eyes and hair like golden silk.

Golden silk?

I'd studied the two photos he'd sent, and from what I could make out, her hair didn't look anything like golden silk to me. It looked like ordinary hair—the kind of hair that anyone would have. Nothing amazing at all.

I tried my best to be pleased for Oscar. When I told my mum about how he was getting to know the girl who was living in my room she asked me if I had any particular feelings about that situation that I might like to talk about.

"What do you mean?" I'd asked her, and for the first time in ages, I felt kind of annoyed, and she said, "It might be difficult for you to hear of someone sleeping in your bed and spending time with Oscar like that."

"I don't know what you're talking about," I replied, slamming my laptop shut, and heading to the door. "And anyway, you're the one who decided to rent out our house. I never thought it was a good idea, and on top of that, it doesn't matter now, I don't even care, because I've loads of friends here. I'm not dependent on Oscar for anything."

"I didn't say you were, it's just—"

"Mum, honestly, I'm fine. I mean, Oscar can hang out with whoever he wants. How could I stop him from doing that? In fact I'm glad. I'm really glad for him. I was worried about how he was going to spend the winter, what he was going to do and now, see, look at that! He's made a new friend and it's great. Really, really glad for him, okay?"

Then I told her I was off to hang out with a bunch of my own new friends at the lake. We might even go water-skiing.

And we did, and then afterward I chatted to Keira and Dougie and a few of the others and I told them about this girl and I wondered aloud if Paloma Killooly or whatever her stupid name was, knew how to water-ski or surf or if she'd ever swum in a lake with black swans gliding nearby and huge craggy mountains looking at her from a clean pale sky.

We sat at a picnic table and I pulled at a few strands of my red hair and I held them in between my fingers and I wondered what I would look like if it was a different color—swan-black say, or golden silk.

"I've done a load of interesting things here that I bet she's never done," I announced to everybody. I wasn't sure why, and neither were they.

"Hey, Meggy, don't fret," Dougie had said. "You'll be going home in a couple of months, and you'll be back in that room and you and Oscar will pick up exactly where you left off."

I often thought about those words afterward, and they used to hit me between the eyes sometimes, as if someone had thrown a big rock straight at my face.

To: Meg Molony
From: PalomaK
Subject: Hellllooooo!!! From YOUR ROOOOOM!!!!!


Dear Meg Molony!!
Oscar Dunleavy has given me your email and so now
I'm writing to you—I hope that's okay!! So as you probably
know, my mother and I are living in your house! And I've
moved into your room!! And I thought it would be nice to
drop you a line to introduce myself seeing as we're gonna
B in the same year at school when you get back!!!! Hope u
enjoyin NZ!!! Have made VERY GOOD friends with Oscar!!!
Isn't that fun? He's fantastic!! Will be so gr8 to meet you too
when u get back!!
PalomaK


PS Please tell me for goodness sake—how does your
shower work? I will never get the hang of it.


She sounded okay, I had to admit. I mean it was a friendly note
and—apart from the exclamation mark overdose—I couldn't really
fault it. She was being nice, and Oscar was always reminding me
that most people are fundamentally decent and that it doesn't pay to
think badly of them. And why wouldn't she make friends with Oscar?
Everyone wanted to be his friend. Nobody in our school didn't want
to hang out with him—and nobody didn't like him. That's the way
he was.

I wrote back to her saying how "gr8" it was to hear from her and
that I was looking forward to meeting her in person too.

The morning after that, there was another email waiting for me:

To: Meg Molony
From: PalomaK
Subject: BTW


I took your mattress off the bed today and guess what
I found under it? Yes! A letter for Oscar!! How did it get
there?!! Anyway, I posted it through his mailbox, okay? No
need to thank me—that's the kind of thing that roomies do
for each other!!! Write back! Let's be pen pals! Wouldn't that
be a laugh? Px

A massive wave of heat flooded through me, followed by what felt like a skewer of ice stabbing me in the stomach. Bloody hell. I tried desperately then to remember the exact words that I'd written, but all I remembered was that it had definitely been my declaration of *love*. And now Oscar was going to read it—that's if he hadn't already. It wasn't Paloma's fault. She'd thought she was being helpful. No one could blame her.

I felt dizzy and a bit sick. Perhaps I still had time, I thought for a moment as the image of Oscar actually *reading* my secret note became more and more clear and more and more mortifying.

I checked the time of her email, thinking for one bright and comforting second that I might still be able to reverse things and persuade Paloma to snatch that letter back before Oscar had had a chance to read it. But no chance, of course. She had sent it over a day ago. He already had my letter, and he knew what was in it and it was too late to do anything except sit blinking at my laptop thinking what kind of damage-limiting thing I should try to do next.

# the eighth slice

A s soon as I'd read it, I'd wished I hadn't.

*Dear Oscar,*

*Just in case you have some idea that you and me could ever be
a couple, I thought you would find it useful to know that that's
never, ever going to happen. I'm not into it and you might as well
get used to realizing that. Maybe it's time for you to move on? Stop
obsessing about one person and look at possibilities elsewhere. It's
okay being your friend and everything. Stop me if I'm making any
assumptions here that I'm wrong about. I just thought I should
be clear with you so you can get on with your life and I can get on
with mine.*

> *What I'm really saying is that you need to spread your wings.*
> *Adios,*
> *Meg*

I lay on my bed then all rigid and tense, letting a thousand
cheerless thoughts chase each other around my head. And then I

heard a noise. It was Paloma throwing those little bits of plaster—plaster she'd found on Meg's sill—at my window and asking me about the letter. I wasn't in the mood to talk about it but Paloma had this way of blinking at me quite slowly, and it made me want to tell her my secrets. And before I knew it, I was confiding in her about how Meg didn't have any interest in . . . well . . . in me. She listened carefully and she nodded her head a lot and went "uh huh, I see, mm." She said she had some advice. She said that the only way to respond to a letter like that was to ignore it completely, and to act as if I didn't care about what it said—as if what it said was totally immaterial and of no consequence to me whatsoever.

"Oscar, you need to let her know that what was in that letter is so irrelevant that you've practically forgotten what it says. That's by far the best way to deal with something like that."

I reckoned Paloma was doing her best to be wise and honest and helpful and I wanted to take her advice.

"I'd say you're better off not thinking about that girl. She doesn't sound too nice," Paloma said, then, which was Paloma's own opinion and possibly fine if you're able to apply logic to a particular situation. But the things I felt about Meg, they didn't operate, they didn't even exist, in the logical, rational part of my brain. Paloma might as well have been telling my heart to stop beating, or commanding my blood to stop flowing through my veins.

After Paloma had said good night, an email pinged into my mailbox:

To: Oscar Dunleavy
From: Meg Molony
Subject: Accidental letter—please disregard.

Oscar, I'm really sorry but Paloma's been in touch and she told me that she dropped a letter from me in(?) to you and yes, it's from me but you weren't supposed to get it and you see I never really meant what I said when I wrote it —I wasn't really thinking. You see, I'm not sure what got into me and not only did I not mean to write it, I definitely never meant for you to get it. It was only a kind of a hypothetical doodle—none of it is really true.

So please disregard. Can you pretend I never wrote it, and that you never read it? Hope that is okay with you. Tell me when you've received this email and we can put the whole thing out of our minds.

Meg

From Oscar Dunleavy
To: Meg Molony
Subject: Accidental letter—please disregard

Meg, I was pretty relieved to get your email. And I'm totally fine about forgetting the letter. To be honest, I was kind of baffled when I first read it, so to hear that you never wanted me to read it in the first place makes a lot of sense. Let's forget it like you suggest. I'm okay with that if you are, and I definitely think it's the best thing to do.

Oh and, Meg, by the way, if I've ever given a wrong impression to you—you know, if I've ever tried to imply something about us in the past, you should forget about that too, because I didn't mean it. I didn't mean to send any wrong message, okay? If I've given you any reason to think that I think about you in a particular way, then I apologize. I never deliberately would have wanted you to get that impression. Let's still be friends, though, because, I mean, that's what we are, isn't it?

    Thanks,

    Oscar

# the ninth slice

Once a letter's been read, you can't unread it. Maybe I should have been reassured to hear that he was happy to do as I had asked, i.e. put the whole thing out of his mind. But I didn't feel reassured. I felt brokenhearted, and I felt rejected, and I felt humiliated. I was the one who had told him to ignore the things I'd told him I'd been feeling about him. So why did I feel like the one who'd been slapped in the face? My secret was out. And his feelings for me, or should I say his non-feelings, were as clear as they could be. I guess I should have been glad to have got there first, to take back the things I'd never meant to say in the letter I'd never meant to send. I wasn't glad at all, though. Whatever the opposite of glad is—that's what I felt.

From then on, something went wrong between me and Oscar. Our friendship got so bent out of shape that I wasn't going to be able to straighten it out. It was never going to be the way it used to be.

> Meg,
> Fantastic news! I'm getting to know Paloma and it's
> great! We have a lot of things in common and loads to talk

about and we sit at the windows like you and I used to, and life hasn't been nearly as much of a drag as I expected it to be. Will keep you posted.

    All the best from your friend,

    Oscar

I got the message.

I kept on wishing I'd never felt those feelings or written them down or slid them under my mattress where Paloma had found them and sent them anyway. But it was too late now.

I tried to forget him but I can't say it was easy. I couldn't shake him off. He was under my skin and little things he said kept echoing around my head. I dreamed of his face and his funny ways and I imagined I could see his bike, twinkling in the moonlight—and sometimes when I was asleep I dreamed of the smell of his apple tarts, even though when I woke up the smell had always gone.

And my parents never seemed to stop talking about how beautifully I was adjusting to New Zealand life. They often said—to anyone who'd listen—how good it was that I wasn't checking Facebook fifty times a day to see what everyone back in Ireland was up to, and how I didn't even seem to need to email Oscar all the time either. For the record, that turned out to be the biggest mistake of my life.

I'd never have predicted I would lose touch with him—before, that is, I did. I thought I had my reasons. But it turns out that they weren't good reasons. It turns out that you should never lose contact with the people who are supposed to be important to you in your life. There is no excuse for doing that.

# the tenth slice

She stopped emailing me and I couldn't get hold of her. And that was exactly the time I really could have done with talking to her because of a whole pile of other things that were happening. The old Meg would have been a massive help. The old Meg would have done her best to get me to figure things out, and everything might have got a good bit better, but I wondered, as the weeks slipped by, whether the old Meg was ever coming back. I began to doubt whether she even existed anymore. When she'd first left, I'd heard from her every single day. Now I hadn't got a single email from her for over a month.

I thought about how I'd kind of assumed that Meg was my person and how stupid I'd been to think that she and I had a fairly excellent future waiting for us when she got back home. And when I realized that I'd been wrong, ridiculously, embarrassingly, shamingly wrong . . . quite rapidly the world went from color to black and white and the magic seemed to drain away and the only thing left for me to do was gather up my personal pride and try to look like the hope I'd had had never existed. I acted as if I wasn't destroyed or defeated. I pretended that I didn't care.

After the letter, everything was different. How could anyone ignore something like that? Maybe some people would be able to, but I couldn't. It's not like I didn't try, but the knowledge of it made its imprint on everything.

It's not as if I didn't have other things in my life: Paloma, for example. She'd been great, and we'd become good friends. At least I thought we had. I guess she was difficult to read sometimes and okay, there were definitely times when I wasn't really sure what to make of her. I'd call in on the way to school and she'd be happy enough to cycle along beside me, chatting away until we got close to the school gates, when she seemed to disappear. Quite often I'd have a hard time catching up with her for the rest of the day.

I'd see her in the yard standing very close up to people like Andy Fewer and Greg Delaney, who used to be pretty good friends of mine too, and I'd wave, and when she looked up or if she saw me heading toward her, she'd have a strange crooked smile on her face and she'd laugh and the three of them would scatter in different directions. And then I'd be waving at thin air, feeling stupid.

She'd made a lot of friends since she'd arrived, and she often liked to have private one-on-ones with them. Most of what she said must have been very funny because people often used to explode with mental-sounding laughter just after she'd whispered something in their ear.

My apple tarts had never seemed to work on my dad, and it's not like I hadn't tried. But no matter how many times I encouraged him to have a slice or two, it didn't seem to make any difference. I reckoned that some people were just immune and there was nothing you could do about it.

But then one night, Dad, Stevie and I were watching this program. It had a celebrity baker on it who wasn't much older than me, and who happened to be showing everyone how to make tarts—apple tarts as it turns out—quite like the ones I made myself. My dad sat up straight and he pointed at the TV and he looked over at me and he smiled.

I hadn't seen him smile for a long time. He told me that *my* apple tarts looked way nicer than the ones on the show, and he said he bet that the ones on the show couldn't possibly taste nearly as fantastic as mine did.

When he went to the kitchen for a cup of tea, Stevie whispered to me that this was a sign. It felt like the first time Dad had said anything in weeks.

Stevie was happy to help, as usual—sieving the flour into our big glass bowl, sitting at the low table I'd set up for him. That night I made four.

Dad said it would be greedy to keep them all to ourselves so why didn't I take a couple into school in the morning, and Stevie thought that was a great idea too.

But I wasn't sure. I'd been kind of careful about keeping my baking skills under the radar when it came to school. You have to be cautious about stuff like that. School is not always the place to show off when it comes to anything unusual— almost anyone will tell you that.

So, just to be safe, I thought I'd check with Paloma before deciding.

Fortunately, that night she was sitting in Meg's window, brushing her hair. When she saw me, she smiled and asked me what the lovely smell was. I thought it was the right time to tell her about my special talent. She was lovely about it. In fact, she said, "Wow, that's very cool."

I asked her whether, in her opinion, people in school would appreciate homemade apple tarts and she smiled and said, "Of course, they would." How rare for a boy of my age to be able to make things like that, and I said I was vaguely worried that people might think it was a bit "different" but she said, "Not in the slightest, why on earth would anyone think that? Definitely bring them in, Oscar—everyone's bound to be *so* impressed."

And her golden hair glimmered in the starlight.

Paloma had been right. I couldn't have imagined a better reaction. Next day, Mr. O'Leary took one of the tarts into the staff room and I left the other one on the table at the top of the classroom.

When he came out he said he had an announcement: "Everyone! I think we have our candidate for the talent showcase!"

The talent showcase is a national competition—schools can put forward whoever they want for whatever skills they think are suitable. Soon, lots of people had had a slice and people were clapping, and saying things like, "Way to go, Oscar!" and people were claiming that we'd certainly win on behalf of the school, which would have been great seeing as the prize was iPads for everyone. So that was fairly exciting, and in the beginning I felt proud to be representing the school doing something that I loved. I knew I had a talent, but I'd never expected anyone would want me to put it on show like this.

Paloma didn't seem to be as happy as I'd have expected her to be. She looked sort of annoyed. She didn't know why everyone was making such a fuss.

"But you *told* me everyone would love the tarts," I said.

"Yeah, well, I was right about that then, wasn't I?" she replied, still not looking too pleased.

Nobody got detention that day, and nobody got any homework, and the teachers spent the whole time looking like they were actually enjoying themselves.

Lots of other good things happened too, like our hockey team got into the semifinal of the regional league for the first time since 1973, and the school choir sang "Ave Maria" so beautifully that it made Mrs. Stockett cry. Happiness is what she said it was, and pride.

"There's magic everywhere today, Oscar!" said Mr. O'Leary as I was heading for home. It wasn't magic, I thought to myself. It was just people being nice to each other and trying their best. I had a secret feeling that the apple tarts had done their trick again, and I should have felt good about that. But when I got home, Dad was just as silent and sad looking as ever. And when I closed my eyes, I could see Meg's face, and I could hear her talking in my head, and I wanted, more than I had ever realized before, to hold on to her, right at the time she seemed to be slipping away.

Hey, Megser!

What's the story? How come you haven't been in contact? Things are going well over here but it would be nice to hear from you. How are your new friends?

In home news, you may be happy to hear that I have been selected for this year's national talent showcase event. I, Oscar Dunleavy, will be representing our school.

Paloma says lots of people would have liked to be selected so I should count myself lucky. She said in fact that she might have liked to use the competition as the opportunity to display these dress designs that she's supposed to be incredibly good at. She reckons that if she hadn't encouraged me to show off my apple tarts in the first place, then other talents might have been in with a chance of being considered. She said that I had had a very handy break and that I should be grateful to her, which I am.

But now she says she doesn't care and that as a matter of fact, she hopes I win. I deserve everything that people with my kind of skill deserve and she has to admit that, after all, the tarts are delicious.

She's helping me with a practice run in front of the whole class. She's very supportive. She really wants me to get it right and spends ages talking to me about it. Andy and Greg learned iMovie over the summer and they're going to do a big interview with me in front of everyone, and so no doubt I will be an Internet sensation before long—ha ha.

Oscar xx

The thing was that Paloma was very impressed with my tarts, and I was glad. What she wasn't too keen on was me being chosen for the talent showcase "just like that" and when she had a chance to explain, I saw that she had a fair point. She'd clicked her long, slender, nail-polished fingers to illustrate how quickly and randomly the decision had been made.

"Surely someone shouldn't be chosen like that without giving other people a chance? Surely everyone should have the opportunity to show what they can do before the winner is selected?"

Mr. O'Leary was insistent.

"Quiet now, Paloma, please," he'd said. "Of course, we don't need a competition; we know who we're going to put forward from class 3R. Oscar. Oscar Dunleavy and his beautiful apple tarts with the exquisite motifs—they are amazing."

"No one ever won a talent competition with *food*," she'd objected.

"Yes, they did," Alison Carthy had butted in. "A guy on *Britain's Got Talent* got through to the live shows with artistic toast."

"Yeah, see, think about how ridiculous that even sounds. Apple tarts are equally weird and our whole class isn't just going to be the laughingstock of the school. If he gets through, the whole bloody world will be laughing at us. It's not fair. Other talented people are in this class. We should at least have a chance to show what we can do."

Later, at the windows, Paloma said she hoped I appreciated where she was coming from. She hadn't meant to disrespect my skill, and she wanted me to realize that it was nothing personal.

"No offense," she'd said. "I'm a hundred percent on your side when it comes to your talent. It's just that somebody needs to stand up for democracy and freedom of speech and fairness for all."

Not bad things to stand up for, I agreed, when I'd had more of a chance to think about it.

# the eleventh slice

He'd promised me that everything was going to be exactly the same. I'd heard him say it, and he'd been looking straight into my face sitting in the window where I thought he was always going to be waiting for me. But Oscar had lied to me and I knew that now, because everything was becoming completely different.

Someone else was in the middle of taking my place, living in my room, hanging out of my window, having huge long conversations with him, helping him with regional talent showcases, and talking to him about apple tarts and competitions and who knows what else, right there in the place where I used to be.

I didn't want to talk to him or email him or send him updates on what was going on. I wanted to punish him, I think. I wanted to punish him for making friends with someone, which goes to show what a horrible person I am. How could I have blamed him for doing that? Oscar was the friendliest guy I'd ever known. It was in his nature to make friends with people, especially new people who were starting at school and didn't know anybody. Newcomers, as everyone knows, are vulnerable and in need of decent treatment.

It was wrong of me to be so jealous. But the sting from those thousands of miles away was sharp and deep and it seemed to harden me and make me turn away from him, which, as I said, is a thing I'd never have predicted I'd have been capable of, until I did it.

Oscar wasn't put off by my lack of communication. He kept on writing, but I knew. I knew how different things had become, and from then on, I felt his sense of duty stamped on the messages he wrote—and that stung me too. He wasn't writing to me because he really wanted to, at least I didn't think he was. He was writing to me because he felt it was the right thing to do, seeing as I was so far away and seeing as he'd said he would.

Oscar, I'd thought bitterly, I don't need your duty. I'm going to show you how much I don't need you. Wait till you see how well I can do without you.

From: Oscar Dunleavy
To: Meg Molony
Subject: Talent show disaster

I'm not sure what's happened, but everyone has turned against my apple tart showcase. Thought you might be able to help me figure it out.

Here's what happened. You'll probably find out sooner or later anyway: practice was in front of the class, and it was so much of an embarrassing disaster that now I'm seriously thinking of not going forward for the competition.

Luckily, Paloma has been working hard on a lot of her designs and she's told me she will be happy to go in my place if I decide not to, which will be the perfect solution, as I don't fancy being the one to let the school down by backing out. I think this could be much better all around really. Not sure why everyone's done such a massive U-turn, but it seems that lots of people have started to think that *nobody* wants to see a kid cooking apple tarts. That could look a bit weird. What do you think?

Paloma is being great and says that maybe I should try to develop a different talent that more people will "get."

Wish you'd write and let me know how you're doing. It would be great to hear from you. Feels like a pretty long time since . . . you know . . . you wrote to me.

Your friend,

Oscar

I wasn't able to stop thinking about the letter he'd accidentally got from me and how bloody *mortified* I was that he'd read it—and how even more completely embarrassed I was about how horrified he'd been at the idea of me being in love with him.

I couldn't blame him for not feeling the same way I did. Of course I couldn't—not logically. You can't force people to feel things they don't feel, or to say things they don't mean. But even though it was unreasonable to be angry with him and even though I tried hard not to be, I was, and it's why, even when I did get around to writing to him, this is what I said:

From: Meg Molony
To: Oscar Dunleavy
Subject: Everything fine, thank you

Hello, Oscar, sorry it's been a while. Hope everything is good and that you and your next-door neighbor continue to have a great time hanging out together. I'm doing really fantastically over here myself, thanks. You wouldn't believe it if you saw the huge bunch of new friends I've made. They're all really, brilliantly good fun. We practically never stop laughing. We go to the lake after school every day and water-ski and have barbecues and whatever we feel like. It's cool. Plus you know, we're so lucky with the climate and the weather and stuff. How's the Irish winter going? Hope it's not too cold or wet or anything.

So, while I'm on the subject of having a great time, the thing is that I'm getting pretty busy, and I don't think it's going to be possible for me to write to you as often as I have been. And I don't expect you to either. Maybe it's time that we both got on with living in our different worlds.

So what I'm saying really is I don't think you should feel any pressure to keep emailing me, okay? It's always been great to hear from you and it's not that I don't love getting emails from you, Oscar, but I have to get on with my life, you know? I simply can't spend my whole time here staring at the screen of my laptop waiting for news from you when the sun is shining outside and I should be doing things to make the most of everything. I have to "embrace the experience," remember? I need to give it a fighting chance over here. New Zealand is my home right now. So . . . I think you'll know what I mean.

Oh and by the way, now that you've asked me about it, I guess I might as well tell you that the apple tart thing *is* a bit strange. So, if you have the chance to opt out, it's probably worth backing out of the talent whatsit. If I were you, that's what I'd do.

Meg

It was cheap and mean of me, I know. Oscar was magic and so were his tarts and everyone should have known that, especially me. But I was jealous and I wanted to hurt him and make him feel small for not liking me. And I didn't want him and Paloma to become the stars of 3R while I was away.

I wish I could take back those things I wrote.

Oscar replied almost instantly, saying he took my point about the tarts but that he didn't have a clue what I meant when I said we shouldn't write. He said he was going to keep writing to me because that's what friends do.

But I wasn't about to change my mind. I got a load more notes from him after that—little thoughts and ideas and reminders of things we'd said to each other. Our windows felt millions of miles away from where I was sitting right then, and the things we'd said to each other were misty to me, and my memories of them were warped and dented because of how far away I felt and because of the stupid letter. That stupid letter. The letter that was never supposed to be sent. The letter I never wanted him to read, especially now that I knew he didn't love me back.

> From: Oscar Dunleavy
> To: Meg Molony
> Subject: Calling Meg. Come in, Meg
>
> Meg? Why have you gone silent on me? Come on, we were supposed to write every day, and now you've gone quiet and disappeared and I could really do with a talk. So stop being mean, open your laptop and send me a photo or

something so I can remember what you bloody well look
like, okay?

I got a few more emails like that from him, but I didn't answer
any of them. The last one I got was four words long. *Meg, where are
you?* was all it said.

Two weeks after that was when the news came.

# the twelfth slice

When I came into school on the first of February, my locker had PERV written in huge letters on it. Permanent black ink. "What the hell?" I said to Andy and Greg, who happened to be hanging around nearby.

Andy said, "We dunno, man, but people don't write stuff like that on your locker for no reason," and Greg said, "You know, Oscar, if you'd liked her, all you had to do was tell her. I mean remember how she was practically offering herself to you at the start?" And then they shrugged their shoulders and I watched them walking away from me, jostling each other along the corridor.

Soon nobody was talking to me. People walked over to the other side of the corridors when they saw me. And they whispered and giggled quite a lot when I was around, and when I asked to borrow Terry Kelly's ruler, she threw it across the room in completely the other direction and someone else caught it and ran off.

I peered into the gym one Thursday after double math to see if class had started, and Brian Dillon walked by and said, "Perving again are we, Oscar?" and I told him I didn't have a clue what he was talking about, and he said, "Yeah right, I bet you don't," and disappeared before I had a chance to ask him what he'd meant.

Amazing how quickly you can turn from an ordinary boy with no distinguishing features, to a weirdo with an apple-tart habit who hardly anyone would talk to.

I'd started to rethink my whole life—even before I knew the truth about myself. And after that . . . when I knew everything, nothing made sense anymore.

I never totally got the hang of jumping out of the window and scaling the tree. But the night I made my drastic decision, I'd flown down it like some lithe creature of the jungle. It's funny what misery and recklessness can do to improve your skills.

I headed as fast as I could toward my bike, which was shining at the gate where I always left it. It was a dark choice I'd made, and it was going to be irreversible, but I got surer and surer that it was what I was going to do. The pier has a massive drop at the end of it, right beside the long rusty ladder that stretches into the deep.

"Meg," I said inside my head, "Meg, do you remember how you and I often dangled our legs at the end of it as the light wilted in the winter evenings and how we wondered what would happen if either of us had fallen?"

And I remember her saying, "We wouldn't last long in that water, not in the wintertime."

I was thinking about that and the pounding in my head was practically unbearable—except for the fact that I'd decided I was going to make it stop.

It only took four minutes and twenty seconds to get from my

house to the bollard at the pier—as long as I cycled fast, making sure to keep my hands off the brakes. Plus there's no traffic in the middle of the night.

I wanted to be emptied of the things that I was full of. I didn't want to be here anymore. A massive knot tightened inside me that was never going to be untied. It was complicated and tangled and I kept telling myself I was sorry, but I couldn't see any other way.

My feet whirled on the pedals and the noise of the chain was calming, like a quiet tune or a reassuring whisper.

"Get out of here," is what it kept repeating, and I kept listening to it because it was extremely convincing, strengthening my decision.

I barreled over Hallow Bridge with its lights that never work properly—always flashing on and off at unpredictable intervals. I kept going until I made it to the top of the lane that led to the pier.

"Good-bye Hallow Bridge," I said stupidly, and then louder— "Good-bye Dad, and good-bye to your agonizing silence and your grief, which I can't *stand* anymore. Good-bye, Meg, not that you'll probably care, seeing as you've moved on and seeing as our friendship doesn't actually matter to you. Good-bye Stevie, I'm really sorry for leaving you, but when you find out about me, as you definitely will one day, then you'll be glad I'm gone too.

"And good-bye Paloma, thanks for being the only one who was brave enough to tell me the truth. Thanks for that. I would say I'll never forget it, but, I'll probably be forgetting everything very shortly— so that will be it."

I couldn't wait for the thudding in my head to stop. I was looking forward to that.

I was looking forward to falling into the black nothing that seemed to be pulling me toward it.

Meg. Meg Molony—I let her name turn around inside my

mouth a few last times. Meg, I'm sorry everything turned out so wrong. It was fairly foolish making a farewell statement that no one could hear, but there wasn't time for a note.

I could hear a strange buzz getting closer and closer and a whistling in the air. I might have lost my hope, but I still had my pride. And I remember thinking, at least that's something—to have pride still. It was a small consolation in the middle of this.

I think I might have even said good-bye to myself as if two people were inside me, which goes to show how mad I had become.

I pushed off the ground and I started to freewheel down. It's a steep lane and I picked up massive speed, which I thought at the time must have explained the almost tuneful whistling that rose above the other noises, piercing through the air. Clattering now and bumping along the uneven ground, I emerged onto the pier, always a kind of startling sight after the walled lane, but this time I could not get pleasure from the twinkle of the stars and the glisten of the water and the slapping of the sea against the rocks, because of my desperation and because these were going to be my final moments, and in situations like that, you don't have time to stop and appreciate your surroundings.

I steered myself as evenly as I could, and it was easier than I thought. My bike and I went shooting off the end, and together we fell into the sea that's cold and huge and doesn't care whether living boys launch themselves into it or not.

A feeling of slow motion came upon me then, and parts of my bike scratched against bits of my body. Slimy seaweed tangled around my ankles and my shoes slipped off my feet. My arms and legs were dragged in different directions as if there was an underwater force making me dance to a morbid tune.

I felt light. I felt heavy. I felt slow. I felt fast—all in quick succession, but I couldn't think of anything except the quite relaxing idea that soon everything was going to be over.

I was alone. All around the wet rocks were silent and slimy. I couldn't feel any pleasure or any purpose. My decision seemed to make a terrible kind of sense.

My panic had gone. I was finished making decisions. I didn't think I'd ever have any more to make.

I'm not sure exactly what I'd been hoping for next. Brightness and song possibly. Beautiful music perhaps, say a harp or something playing in the distance and warmth to soothe my numb, frozen, sopping, scraped body.

I definitely wasn't expecting what happened next.

I heard a voice and this time it wasn't coming from inside my head. I felt hands, hands that were not mine—trying to grapple with me—trying clumsily to lift me up.

"So this is what it's like," I said to myself, shivering pretty violently, but not feeling scared anymore. "It feels as if someone is carrying me and bringing me somewhere safe. That's not so bad."

The hands laid me down on uncomfortable, bumpy ground, and a voice of velvet and sand spoke to me soft and low.

It was Barney. Barney Brittle. Naturally I asked him what on earth he was doing and he asked what did it look like he was doing, which was rescuing me from a watery end. He said that not so long ago, I'd saved him and he explained that what goes around comes around—now it was his turn to save me, so here he was, soaking wet because of how he'd jumped in to get me out. He may have been dripping and he may have looked kind of grim and desperate but he was stubborn too and there was something strong about the way he looked at me. I was weak and freezing. I thought I had known what I was doing but I had not.

He reminded me that he himself had been very frightened on this same spot, once, not so long ago. He told me he knew exactly what it was like to feel what I was feeling, and he didn't envy me. But now he said that I didn't have to think about another thing for the moment, because he was calling the shots. He was the one who was going to decide what happened next, which suddenly was okay with me. At that particular moment I would have followed him anywhere.

As it happens, following him was more difficult than I might have imagined. He had a sort of fearsome way of walking. At first he'd suggested he could carry me on his shoulders, which I said wouldn't be necessary. He hurried at an improbably fast pace through the maze of back streets that weave through my town and reached a wall at the top of Primrose Hill.

I must have passed the same wall a million times and never noticed the thin little gate that was set into it, overgrown with brambles and creepers. He opened it and looked around as if he was worried someone might be following us. We squelched up a twisty, narrow path with walls on either side that kept getting higher and higher, and he kept talking to himself in a way that was definitely a bit weird.

"Where are we?" I asked him. He told me that we were on the way up to his house, and the couple of times I checked with him, he reassured me that I wasn't actually dead.

He told me it was a poor choice for a suicide if that's what I had been trying to commit. I told him I hadn't had a heck of a lot of time to think it through, that I'd planned it in a tremendously short space of time, under what you might call extreme pressure.

"I'm happy to say that you made an ineffective decision. You're most unlikely ever to have topped yourself using the strategy you'd selected."

I was getting a bit out of breath trying to keep up with him.

"Somewhere he can shelter," he said, whispering and wheezing a bit, but not slowing for a second. "Somewhere he can get warm, and where no one can find him. Don't mess it up, Barney. This boy is falling. You must catch him."

Barney's house stood battered and gloomy, as if it was in a sulk from having gone to the elaborate trouble of being built and then having been neglected so badly that it looked as if nobody lived in it.

# the thirteenth slice

I'd been at the lake after school. It was the first Thursday in February, two minutes to six. My mum was holding a huge glass bowl full of salad. She answered the phone and as she listened, her wrist dropped and her hand slipped, and tons of balsamic vinegar started spilling over the edge of the bowl, making a massive black puddle on the floor.

And I was like, "Mum, watch out, you're pouring dressing all over the place," but she wasn't listening, obviously, because not only did she not watch out, she then dropped the entire bowl. Lettuce was by my feet, and tomatoes rolled around, and there was the rumbling noise of the bowl, which trundled around the kitchen as if it had a mind of its own.

My mum did a strange small intake of breath that people sometimes do when they know something's terribly wrong, even before they know exactly what that something is.

It had been Mr. Dunleavy. He and my mum had spoken for a long time. Or should I say he'd spoken, and my mum had listened silently, her face growing a blue kind of pale that I'd never seen before. After she'd said good-bye, she asked me to come and sit down at the table, and I said I wanted to have a shower first. But she wrapped a big towel around me and said the shower could wait.

She told me then about how Oscar's bike had been pulled out of the water and how they'd found his shoes.

"Okay," I'd said, "let's not panic. Maybe he left the bike too close to the edge. He's very careless with that bike. And I can't tell you the number of times he goes off on his own without telling anyone. But he always comes back. Maybe he just lost the shoes because he went for a swim."

"Darling? In February? No, he didn't go for a swim. Meggy, I'm really sorry to tell you but you see, there's a massive search under-way, and, sweetheart, it's been a few days already and I'm afraid people have begun to think the worst."

"The worst?" I said, looking up at her. "What does that mean?" Which was a stupid question because obviously I knew what it meant.

My hair was dripping. I wanted to walk back out of the house with my hands over my ears. I wanted to go back to the moment, not long before, when I was in the water myself, happy and clueless, and unaware of Oscar's sopping wet bicycle and the search party and the days that had already slipped by—days that didn't have Oscar in them. Suddenly I felt like a whole different person.

I ran up to my room and clicked frantically on my laptop.

There was a pile of unread email. Andy Fewer. Rob Delaney. Stevie. And there was one from Paloma. Paloma Killealy. Her email said how devastating the situation was and asked if I could do anything to shed light on what had happened to Oscar because if I could, I was to tell her straightaway, even though she explained this was unlikely seeing as how I'd been so far away and seeing as me and him obviously weren't really as close as we'd been in the past.

Stevie's email said, "Meggy. Have you heard the news? Please come home. I need to talk to you. If I could talk to you, we'd be able to find him. Don't let anyone try to convince you he's dead. Because he's not, Meggy. He can't be. Come home. I really need to see you. Love Stevie."

I checked the last email from Oscar. It had been two weeks before. How can it have been that long? I dragged up Facebook. Not a single post from him for over a month. And now this news. It felt as if a blunt object was repeatedly whacking me in the face. Oscar Dunleavy had disappeared. Nobody could find him. Nobody knew where he was. He was gone.

"Oscar, my mum says you've done a runner somewhere." I clacked a frenzied message to him. "Tell me it's not true will you please, straightaway? Oscar, seriously, you've got to get in touch."

The words began to tremble in front of my eyes. More messages popped up in my inbox. Mr. O'Leary. Stevie again.

Oscar's dad had sent a frightening list of questions:

When did he last write to you?

Did you notice any changes in him?

What had he talked about recently?

Did he mention going away, or maybe he told you about something he was planning to do?

Was he behaving out of character?

Is there somewhere that he goes that we might not know about?

Might he be staying in a place that you know about?

The questions went right to the bottom of the page, each as impossible to answer as the one before, each of them screaming a message of growing panic. A fire was in my head when I ran back to the kitchen where both my parents were on their phones talking in serious, hushed tones and mumbling things that I could not hear.

"I never wanted to come to New Zealand!" I shouted. "I told you a thousand times but you wouldn't listen to me. I didn't want to leave my life behind. I didn't want to leave Oscar, and now, *now* look what's bloody well happened."

They probably should have told me to stop, but they didn't say a single word—not even when I picked up a mug and threw it on the floor.

If someone who is a friend of yours goes missing, it's important that you go home to recognize what they meant to you. You have to go back to the places where they last were to find out what happened.

It was funny how much work Mum and Dad had done to get me over here, and now we were going to go home anyway, because of Oscar. And for a short while, I'd wondered if I was going to have to have a big fight about it, but I didn't even have to say a word. My parents had agreed that getting home and paying respects to Oscar's dad and to Stevie were more important things to do than for my dad to finish his time here.

"Sometimes things happen and you need to jettison your own priorities," he'd said to me. I was glad that my parents knew it was the right thing to do. They'd already booked the flights. Two days later, we were packed and the details had been taken care of.

A big part of Dad's research project got handed over to this guy called Jerry Nolan. I said sorry, but Dad said I wasn't to give it another thought. This wasn't my fault, he said, and I didn't have the heart to start explaining how much of it was. He went on about how research projects would come and go, and that none of that mattered right now because they wanted to focus on me, and how I was feeling.

I loved my dad even in the confusing mist that surrounded me during those days. My mum kept stroking my forehead as if I was a really small kid. It was a little bit annoying and not much help or anything, but I didn't say a word to her about it because when someone is trying to comfort you they sometimes need to do quite useless annoying things and you shouldn't stop them.

And for the whole time, nobody asked me to do anything. They didn't get cross with me if I didn't answer them. They stopped giving me the usual instructions, such as pick up after yourself or do your homework or brush your hair. The one time I could have done with a few mundane activities to take my mind off things, was the one time they let me sit in the corner doing nothing.

A couple of my Kiwi classmates called in to say good-bye. They stood around looking awkward and some of them said stuff such as how sorry they were to have heard about my best friend back in Ireland. That was no comfort either, even though I knew they were trying to be nice. They didn't know Oscar.

The things that were in my head were wrapped up, muffled and distant and I couldn't talk to anyone about them. Mostly I sat on my own trying to imagine what I was going to say to everyone when I got back. I was glad when it was time to get a taxi to the airport.

New Zealanders are probably the most cheerful people on the planet. When you've heard that your best friend is missing, being surrounded by cheerful people is enough to drive you insane. My parents drew a protective circle around me, telling me they were here for me and they loved me and that everything was going to be okay. But everything was not okay, and everything was never going to be okay ever again.

We got home on a gray morning. The rain was like pins on my face and the wind wrapped itself around me like an unpleasantly damp blanket doing the opposite of what blankets are supposed to do. Paloma and her mother were still living in our house so we had to rent an apartment.

Paloma's mum left flowers in the hall of our new place, and a note saying how sorry they were that we had to cut the trip short, and asking were we absolutely sure that we didn't need the house back, and how awful the circumstances of our return must feel. My parents kept going on about what lovely people Mrs. Killealy and her daughter seemed to be.

My new temporary room was so bare it had an echo. My hoodies were packed up in some storage unit. I didn't even have a cardigan. I walked past my old house and glanced up at my window to see if I could see her. I peered into Oscar and Stevie's house, and I looked over at our cherry tree and up at Oscar's window too where the curtains were drawn and the light was off. The chill of his absence was like a big stone, and I had to turn my face away.

# the fourteenth slice

**B**arney had asked me to start from the beginning.

"The beginning of what?" I asked him, and he said, "Try to think of when things started to go wrong. Go back to the moment when you set off along this path, this path where you, you fine young fellow, you charming boy, thought a good option would be to drown yourself in the sea. Have a think about it before you start talking. I have plenty of time."

And he rustled around the cluttered living room with the big, soft, broken sofa in the middle of it, and he sat in another big chair right next to it and looked straight at me. He had no computer or phone or iPad or even a TV as far as I could see. Towers of dusty books surrounded us.

I could feel something that I hadn't felt for a long time. Something quiet and difficult to spot, but it was the feeling that you get when someone is listening to you. Really listening carefully. And it makes you want to tell things exactly the right way. It makes you want to take your time and explain and get it right.

I told him how much I'd missed Meg, but also how Paloma Killealy was a great new arrival in the neighborhood, and how everybody liked having her around and how nice her hair was and how everyone thought she was beautiful.

"Okay, then, let's start with Paloma," he'd suggested, which I supposed was as good a place as any.

"I may have taught her a lot of stuff that I am quite good at explaining, but she taught me a lot too.

"In particular, the thing that sticks in my mind most is what she told me when she first arrived about a thing called The Ratio. It's a useful thing for anyone to be aware of, and if it hadn't been for her, I'd never have known about it."

"The Ratio?" said Barney, quietly building up the little fire, slowly placing sticks in a pile and then balancing a big wooden block on top of them.

"Yes," I replied. "The Ratio. Paloma knew a lot about it because she'd moved a total of seven times since she started school. You learn stuff when you move around like that. Not everyone knows about The Ratio, but it's always the same—no matter what school you go to."

Paloma said it was kind of a universal rule. If you've ever been at school, like ever in your whole life, you should have some inkling, some vague idea that it exists.

For any class of average size, this is roughly the way it goes:

There'll usually be four or five alphas: top dogs, people like Andy and Greg, she told me. They'll walk in slow motion, like astronauts, and they never have to move out of anyone's way. Their lockers are always closest to the door. They don't have to wait in the queue and everyone looks at them when they pass by. Each of the alphas has one or two hangers-on. Nobody really quite understands what's in it for the hangers-on, but they are faithful and true in the way that alphas don't ever seem to deserve.

Invisibles are another group: around seven smart, decent,

quiet, good kids who no one takes much notice of and whose names Paloma predicted everyone would forget within a year of leaving school. And then the "actives" are five cheerful souls who never seem to notice the underbelly that lurks like a watchful reptile in every class. They throw themselves into ten-kilometer runs and colors days and events designed to make school look like a wholesome, simple, happy, straightforward place.

There are three or four serious messers—their sequence on the ladder changes daily: they'll lose their popularity in a split second by flicking a spitball at some target, and accidentally hitting Andy Fewer.

There is a small bunch of outliers: the punky, kohl-eyed, T-shirted, pink-haired, black-booted, notebook-writing, music-listening crew, never quite knowing where they fit in and not being sure if they ever want to.

And that's pretty much it. Except for one more. One other person. The person on the bottom. Nobody wants to be a member of this sad little one-man club, but somebody always is.

"Sounds complicated," I'd said.

"That's because it is," she'd replied. "Knowing The Ratio is vital," she claimed.

"Is it?" I asked her. I told her that our class was not like that. Everyone got on with each other. We didn't have any outliers and certainly nobody who was the "bottom one."

"Oh yes, you do," she said, "or if you don't, you will."

"Are you sure?"

"Yes, I am," she replied.

Even as we spoke, I'd already started to worry that I might be missing something. I kept suggesting that maybe The Ratio existed in other places, like the places she had been, but I hadn't seen any evidence of it here. And I remember she'd slid a flat stick of chewing gum out of its foil and pointed it at me as if it was a wand, to help emphasize the next bit of the lesson.

"Oscar, you're wrong. The Ratio is everywhere. You need to challenge every single one of the things you think are true. There are surface impressions and then there's the reality that sits beneath that surface. Someone like you might be innocent enough to think that studying math and English and science and geography and history are the most important things you need to do to get ahead at school. That's probably what you've been told.

"But listen to me, Oscar, I'm doing you a massive favor by telling you what I know: it's much, much more important to study The Ratio. That's what you really need to understand. It's where the power lies: it's all about who you can afford to annoy, and who you can't. Where you are, and how likely you are to move. How stable your position is. At the moment, that's up in the air for me because this is the beginning—because I'm new.

"You may think that a casual conversation with a harmless-looking person is of no consequence, but you've got to be incredibly careful. The decisions you make matter. They matter very much. And if you get in too deep, it's difficult to go back.

"No one's going to be able to help you if you get stuck in the wrong category. Look at me, Oscar," she said, and she held me by the shoulders and I could feel her slender fingers kind of digging into me—she spoke as if this was the most important thing I was probably ever going to learn.

"These things do *not* work themselves out. This will not pass. Do take notice. Take a *lot* of notice. This is the rest of your *life* we're talking about. This is not something simple."

"So are you studying the form at the moment? Have you placed everyone in one of your categories already?"

"Me? Oh goodness no, Oscar," Paloma replied, using this old-fashioned kind of voice and raising her perfect eyebrows in a high, indignant arch.

"This is the world order I'm talking about. This doesn't come from *me*! Come on, I wouldn't take it on myself to label anyone in that way. All I'm saying is that's what people do. But me? Don't you know me by now? Can't you see that I just want to be everyone's friend?"

Barney said that in his opinion, a thing like The Ratio only existed if people believed in it.

"I know," I replied. "I mean, I had completely thought that too. At first I'd thought she had it wrong. I thought she was applying some random set of rules to her new environment, the same way she had when she thought boys were supposed to take girls to The Energizer and stuff like that. I kept trying to tell her that The Ratio didn't exist here, but she kept telling me that it did. It was every-where, she said; it's basically the way human beings work.

"And you see, Barney, it turns out she was right. It turns out that there'd been a vacancy for the Person At The Bottom, and not long after she'd briefed me about it, I was the one who filled it. I must have been the naivest person on the planet—thinking that everyone got along with everyone else—liking the people in my class and assuming that they liked me. But our links with one another had been damaged and poisoned somehow, and it's funny, but no sooner had Paloma told me about The Ratio, than I started to notice it. You see, Barney, coincidentally, it was right then that everything started to go wrong."

"Doesn't sound like a coincidence to me," said Barney.

Barney said that everyone must be worried. But I'd put my head in my hands, then, and I'd said, "Please, please don't make me go back."

That's when he said I could stay as long as I wanted.

"No pressure in the slightest, my dear boy," is what he said.

And so I started living in his house, which was the messiest house I'd ever been in, in my entire life.

After a couple of nights I got used to hearing him leaving late at night when he thought I was asleep, and in the mornings he always had new information, not that I was too thrilled to hear some of it—seeing as it was about posters with my face on them and newspaper articles about my disappearance. I was interested in the Day of Prayer for Oscar Dunleavy they'd had, though. Barney'd said that everyone in my class had been right up at the front and how everyone had said how terrible it was that I had gone.

"Oh right," I said, trying to sound uninterested, "and did you hear anything else?"

"Yes. I heard that everyone liked you enormously."

"Yeah," I said, "maybe some people did. Maybe they meant in the past, before everything changed. Anyway, it's easy for people to like you when you're dead. It's a pity none of them could see their way to liking me when it mattered to me, when I was alive."

"You're still alive, Oscar. You're not dead. Had you forgotten?"

"Look, I don't want to talk about whether I'm alive or dead, and I don't want to talk about my old life. I don't want to talk about any of that."

"Why not?"

"Because I am ashamed," I said.

# the fifteenth slice

In the weeks that followed, I tried to confront Paloma Killealy, but it didn't take a genius to figure out she was trying to avoid me. She and I were in the same year, in the same school. We walked along the same corridors, went through the same doors, ate in the same lunchroom. It seemed impossible that I wouldn't come face-to-face with her. But I hadn't—not since Oscar's mass. I could only assume she was deliberately avoiding me and I wouldn't have blamed her. I would have avoided myself too if I could have.

Now my only connection with Oscar was Stevie. He used to make me smile, particularly as he was the one person who kept believing that Oscar was still alive.

As the days went by, I felt the need to be close to all the gigantic hope that Stevie held inside his small body. Sometimes I'd call by, and Oscar's dad would let me into the house. But other times I'd go around there very late when I knew Stevie'd be in his room, with his candle always dancing in the window. I'd tap on the window and we could end up chatting there for hours.

It was nearly a month after I'd been home that my mum caught me creeping back home on a school night, and naturally enough she wanted to know what I was doing, and where I had been and what I thought I was up to. And then before I had a chance to answer, she said it was too late even to think about having a proper conversation about it now, but next day, me and her and my dad were going to have to have a serious talk.

I snapchatted Stevie to say I was in trouble for sneaking out of my house, and he said he'd be the fall guy for me if that would do any good.

My mum said that my obsessive need to talk to Stevie was not good for either of us, and she told me that I needed to see the grief counselor at school, and that if I didn't set it up, she'd ring Mr. O'Leary herself, so I went okay, okay, I'll do it.

ANYONE WISHING TO RECEIVE EMOTIONAL/
PSYCHOLOGICAL SUPPORT WITH RESPECT TO THE OSCAR
DUNLEAVY TRAGEDY CAN SIGN UP FOR A COUNSELING SESSION
IN THE LILAC ROOM WITH MISS KATY COLLOPY BA PSYCH, ICA.

1 HOUR PER SESSION
TUESDAYS 10–2 P.M. FIRST
COME, FIRST SERVED

said the sign on the notice board outside the Lilac Room.

Mr. O'Leary and Mrs. Stockett both told me how helpful Katy Collopy was likely to be. She had been hired after Oscar had disappeared to help the students to "process their feelings" about the situation, and she'd already been a superb support to lots of people in the class, many of whom were understandably cut up about Oscar.

That watery noise was in my head again, this time accompanied by a kind of a banging, and even though I'd originally had no intention of talking to any counselor or anybody else for that matter, the last thing I wanted was my mum coming into school and talking to people about me and my emotional condition.

In double chemistry, Mr. Grimes was acting as if life was supposed to be going back to normal, and everyone was getting ready to explore the heat-induced reactive properties of aluminum, using empty cans. People seemed disproportionately excited. Raymond Daly leaned over our preparation materials and whispered to me that Paloma Killealy had been the first to sign up for a session with Katy Collopy. I couldn't wait any longer after that, so I scraped back my chair and walked out of the classroom without asking permission. Nobody shouted after me or asked me where I thought I was going. I walked along the shining corridor that led through the push-bar double doors to the basketball court. I started to run across it, and straight to the Lilac Room to look at the sign-up sheet for myself. Raymond Daly had been right. Paloma's name was written carefully on the first line:

## Paloma Killealy

Even her signature was beautiful, tall, fluid and dreamy.

And then I saw her coming out, holding a tissue to her mouth, her head bent. I tried to get a proper look, seeing as I'd only ever seen her from a distance before now. She stood in front of me for a few seconds looking through me, and then she slipped off in her usual mysterious way, with a shadow of sadness falling across her annoyingly beautiful face.

I sat in the waiting chair staring after her as she disappeared. I wasn't going to shout *Hey, Paloma, Paloma come here, I want to talk to you.* Because I was feeling bad enough as it was.

Just then the door of the Lilac Room opened and Katy Collopy said, "Meg? Hello there, Meg. Come on in."

Beanbags lolled around all over the place, and wicker shelves sat full of books with pictures of badly dressed children on them. The books had titles like *How Can I Be Me?* and *Talking to Your Teenager.*

It was kind of gloomy, and there was a cluster of electric fake candles on the shelf, their pretend flames pulsing away and throwing spooky little shapes on the walls.

Katy Collopy smiled a deliberate kind of a smile and slowly pulled at a huge red beanbag and then pushed it toward me with her foot. On it remained the full actual shape of Paloma Killealy.

"Okay, first, Meg, you need to relax, you need to get comfortable." I sat with a gigantic crunch, to crush away the silhouette of that girl.

"Tell me," she asked, after a huge, uncomfortable silence. "Did you know Oscar Dunleavy?"

"Did I know him? What do you mean did I know him?"

"I mean did you talk to him? Was he someone that you knew?"

"I am Oscar Dunleavy's best friend."

"Oh," she said, looking at a yellow notebook and flicking through it. "Were you?"

"Yes, I am, and the reason I'm here is to see if you might be able to help me figure out what kinds of things I need to do if I want to find him."

"Now, Meg," said Katy and her voice got deep and unexpectedly stern. "I'm not sure that would be a fruitful way to use our time. I think it would be better if you and I talked about what's going on in your head, what you're thinking, Meg, what you're feeling.

"The last thing I think you need is to go on a wild-goose chase for Oscar, because we all know that would be futile, don't we? So, Meg, come on, I think it would be helpful for you to talk to me about your emotions."

I looked into her face.

"Well, you know, Oscar's gone. Disappeared. And I am his friend, I mean I was, I mean, I am. I am the one who knew everything about him, but for some reason it's Paloma who everyone is worrying about and taking care of, like I'd never existed—like me and Oscar were some meaningless thing that hadn't signified anything. It's as if Paloma Killealy has been here forever and I haven't been here at all. And on top of that, she's moved into my house, my *room* and at night she goes to sleep in my *bed*.

"It was always me who'd been in that room. That's *my* window. Those were *our* conversations. They didn't belong to anyone else."

I told Katy Collopy that I'd started to hear watery sounds in my head and how every night I'd dream about the bollard and the dripping bike and Oscar's sopping shoes. And sometimes I dreamed that the bollard was speaking. You know, saying something very quietly and that if only I could get near enough, I'd be able to hear.

With an elegant clearing of her throat she said that me hearing the watery noise and dreaming of the bollard represented something significant and understandable. She explained that the mystery of Oscar's final moments must be so important for me to try to understand that I had started to *wish* the stone, which had been the only witness to his anguish, could talk to me. And she said that sometimes when you wish for something very hard, it can kind of come true inside your own head, and it can seem real.

I told Katy Collopy that if her theory was correct, then a lot of other things would be coming true inside my head too and that they'd be a heck of a lot nicer than a big stone whispering things to me in the middle of the night.

"Were you still friends with him when he died?" she asked, still looking a bit confused.

"Look, first," I said, "nobody has any proof that he's dead so I wish you'd stop saying that, okay? And, secondly, ask anyone in my class and they'll tell you that me and him are best friends. We've been best friends for basically years."

"Gosh, all right, I'll take your word for it, so now go on, keep going, tell me what's on your mind."

Katy was good-looking and she had perfect skin, and I suddenly got a strong feeling that no hint of loss had ever cast any pain into the bright corners of her life. And I looked into her clear eyes and the whites of them were really white, almost blue, and her eyelashes were sweepy and perfect, and I think it was something about those eyelashes that made me realize what a waste of time this talking was. Katy was never going to be able to help.

"Meg, I understand, I really do. Especially now that you've told me Oscar had been your best friend."

"He *is* my best friend, I keep telling you. The two of us are really close. But then Oscar is everyone's friend. Speak to anyone in my class. They'll tell you the same things about him. They'll tell you how great he is, how everyone loves him, how there isn't a single person who doesn't like him. And it isn't only my class. He is the most popular boy in the whole school."

A long silence swelled between us like a bubble.

She shook her head slightly and she smiled a sad, frowny kind of a smile.

"How long have you been away, Meg?" she asked me then, and I told her.

"And how often were you in contact with Oscar during that time?"

I told her every day at the beginning, but hardly at all at the end, and a fresh wave of secret guilt crashed over me, and I asked her why she was asking me so many questions.

"Because, Meg, none of this is tallying with the things I've been told about Oscar."

"What do you mean?" I asked.

"Oscar had become a desperately unhappy boy."

"He wasn't unhappy. He was fine."

"Oh dear," she said, leaning forward on her elbows. "He was deeply troubled and depressed."

"No he wasn't! He was happy and lighthearted, and full of joy."

"Was he? Are you sure about that? The facts suggest otherwise."

"The facts? What facts?"

"Motherlessness. Paternal unemployment. Sibling disability. Those things alone represent a big complicated soup of difficulty if you ask me."

"Okay, when you put it like that, when you say those things together it sounds bad but . . . he told me everything. If he was going to *kill* himself, bloody hell, if he was going to do *that*, I know he would have talked to me, he would have told me about it first."

"Can you really know that, Meg? I'm trying to get you to think rationally—to stop holding on to false hope when you need to try to come to terms with this. It's not helping you."

I was sick of talking. I looked out of the window and tried to think about something else.

"Meg," said Katy Collopy, clearing her throat again for another important announcement. "I think it's time that you knew about some of the things that happened after you left. People were treating Oscar extremely badly. I understand he was subjected to a certain amount of pressure. And Oscar was keeping a lot of things to himself. It's common for teenage boys to keep their troubles out of sight—sealed inside themselves until they become too much to cope with. Don't you think he might have been putting his best foot forward—not telling people about the things that were bothering him because he didn't want people to be worried—because he wanted everyone to be happy?"

Suddenly I felt pathetic. It wasn't only that I'd declared my stupid love for him in that stupid letter. It was so many other things too. Bending his ear in the way I had about my trivial problems, when the whole time he was carrying proper real-life burdens. It made me feel like an idiot.

I wished more than ever before that he would walk back in through the door, so I could tell him I was sorry about how selfish I must always have seemed.

Katy was still talking.

"And so you see, Meg, you have to keep in mind the stuff that had happened at school."

"What stuff?"

"How miserable school had become for him—the things I've been trying to explain to you."

"How do you know he wasn't happy at school?"

"I've spoken to other people in the class."

"Who? Who have you spoken to?"

"Oh goodness, Meg, I'm a counselor. You know I can't disclose things like that to you, but you see, there is what's known as the rough and tumble of normal teenage interaction. Teasing and a little bit of mocking. Mean slogans painted on lockers—things like that. Some people are fragile even though they might not appear to be on the outside. As I understand it, what started out as a bit of what I like to call 'joshing,' ended up being something nastier. It turned into a form of toxic humiliation. We can't quite identify anyone in particular who was at fault. These things evolve sometimes, and once they've set in, they're difficult to do anything about."

"You've got to tell me what you're talking about," I whispered. "I need you to explain. I am his friend," I said, hammering on my chest and trying but failing to get out of the stupid beanbag, feeling like a beetle who'd been flipped over on its back. I stayed in a half-lying, half-sitting position feeling helpless and stupid.

"There's no logic to the things that happen to precipitate these kinds of situation—but in Oscar's case, one of the main triggers seems to have been to do with apple tarts. Oscar used to make apple tarts, you see."

"I *know* he did. Of course, I know that. What's that got to do with anything?"

"Well, apparently, a few people began to mock him because he brought them to school."

"Why would they mock him? Those apple tarts were delicious! And they were magic. They cured people of all sorts of things! I can't understand why people would make fun of him about that."

Katy held up one of her beautiful index fingers, looked very carefully at me, and said, "Meg, you see it wasn't simply the tarts, it was something else too. A rumor had begun to go around that Oscar had been behaving, shall we say, quite inappropriately."

"What does that mean?"

So then Katy Collopy told me there'd been this story doing the rounds—that Oscar had been using his telescope to peer into Paloma Killealy's room at night while she was undressing. He'd been stalking her, and the word got out, and because everyone had come to be very fond of Paloma, a lot of people took her side—felt quite protective about her. And also, because nobody could actually *prove* that Oscar was a pervy stalker, they pounced on other things about him, and the apple-tart thing was the obvious target, and that was the excuse everyone used to start making his life a misery: scrawling nasty graffiti on his locker, whispering about him and building this campaign to stop him from representing the school in the talent showcase.

"So it was Paloma, then," I said. "I *knew* it. I knew she was at the center of this—his so-called new best friend who's supposed to be devastated because he's disappeared—and the whole time it was her spreading stupid lies about him. Who else, who else was involved? Who else tormented him so much that he's . . . he's . . . gone . . . ?"

"Please, Meg," said Katy with her infuriating calm voice. "This is a confidential space. As I keep telling you, if I started to disclose who said what to me then I would be transgressing one of the fundamental rules of counseling and I am not prepared to do that. I've told you this in confidence because I think you need to know that things can be more complicated than they seem.

"And another important thing that you need to keep in mind is that Paloma has been through an awful lot, and I don't want you making things more difficult for her. She's been quite brave, you know. Have you heard how well she rallied when it came to the talent showcase?"

I said no I hadn't.

"You see, when Oscar disappeared, somebody had to take his place and Paloma's a wonderful designer and we persuaded her to step in. And at first she said no she couldn't possibly, what with the trauma of losing Oscar, but eventually, remarkably, she said yes. She went forward with four fashion designs—she even modeled one of them herself—so elegant, so graceful, so creative. She did an excellent job, performing like that in front of the judges only a few days after Oscar disappeared. And you'd never even have known how much the loss of him was affecting her. Honestly, you'd never have known how upset she was. Everyone said it."

"Maybe that's because she wasn't that upset," I suggested.

"Don't be silly. Paloma adored Oscar. And Oscar adored her. That's one thing I'm absolutely clear about. They had become very close. It wasn't her fault that he had a more . . . well . . . a kind of . . . obsessive interest in her. She recognizes that. She says she's come across this before. Apparently lots of boys develop very strong feelings for her."

"Oh shut up," I said as I finally managed to stand up.

A small flicker of something furious flashed for a second across Katy's face but then she got calm and composed again and she smiled her tight smile, looked at her watch and said that our time was up.

"Meg, perhaps you want to come back for another session or two, but to be honest, I'm not sure how much more help I can give you," she said coolly.

"No," I said, "neither am I."

Katy went on some more about being a qualified counselor and how in her professional opinion the possibility of Oscar being alive was remote. She said that my hope was a "form of denial" and that in her professional experience such denial could be destructive. And I tried to keep control of my voice.

"Hope is never destructive," I said. "Hope is the thing that keeps you going." I really meant it. You need hope as surely as you need to breathe air and drink water. Without it every one of us might as well fling ourselves off the pier into the murky sea below.

I couldn't talk anymore, and I was a bit scared of what Katy had said to me. I straightened out my clothes that had got twisted up while I had been sitting talking to her.

"I still don't understand how any of this nonsense could have made him so miserable. How could he have got that much despair just because of a bunch of stupid rumors—and in less than six months?"

I stared at some of the brittle things inside the room—the

lightweight wicker table that slid around whenever I touched it, the glittery flecks that shot around the room from the gleam of Katy's diamond ring, the uncomfortable beanbag that had been impossible to sit on.

And I saw the whole situation for what it was: clumsy and uneasy and pointless—talking to a total stranger about things I couldn't bear and didn't want to believe.

Katy said she hoped I'd be all right.

"Remember, just because you were his friend, doesn't mean that any of this is your fault. You can't hold yourself responsible for it. You mustn't," she instructed me. "Lots of people know how you feel, and everybody understands what's going on for you at the moment." I seriously doubted that, but the hour was up, and I wanted to get out.

"Thanks," I said. "Thanks for that."

I walked, kind of frozen, kind of shocked and silenced, back to the classroom. By now Mr. Grimes had got everyone to light these scientific blowtorches for the classroom experiment that had been causing so much excitement earlier.

Small fiery roars of blue flame were bursting in front of everyone, casting a strange new kind of light on the members of my class.

"Is anybody here going to tell me what the hell happened to him? He was perfectly fine when I left and now these stupid rumors have been spread about him and everyone's been teasing him and rejecting him and people think he's *dead*? Come on!" I shouted, trying to lift my voice above the spitting and popping of the torches.

In a single mystified movement, their goggles turned toward me. And suddenly they didn't look like ordinary people anymore. They looked like uniformed demons with frightening expressions, and faces I did not recognize.

# the sixteenth slice

"What could you possibly be ashamed of, my dear boy?" asked Barney, looking astonished.

"Lots of things. Everyone in school suddenly thought I was an idiot. Part of it was people getting the wrong idea about me and Paloma, but part of it was to do with the fact that I'm a loser. I just didn't know it until recently. Everyone stopped wanting to be friends with me, including Meg. I don't blame her or anything. If I was her, I wouldn't want to be friends with me either. Not anymore.

"Meg sent me this letter explaining certain things in it, which made me feel like a fool too. I couldn't get them out of my head. I tried to put it behind me, but it was hard. The only person who'd talk to me anymore was Paloma, and even though she was a bit weird to me when we were at school, she kept on being nice to me in the evenings when she'd talk to me from Meg's window. I mean really nice. Friendly and stuff.

"People started to hate me. It got so that whenever anyone said my name it was as if they were spitting something bad out of their mouths. And for a long time I didn't know why. But I know now."

Barney said that no boy deserved to be turned on that way, especially not someone like me. Talking about it, even thinking about it made me feel as if I might start to cry. Barney said we didn't have to discuss it anymore if it was going to upset me.

He and I got used to each other and to spending the afternoons together. He had a massive old garden in the back and it seemed as if everything in his life was tangled and twisted and that he couldn't sort out one thing from another. His house was disgusting.

Together we tried to straighten everything up. Barney wasn't poor, even though he totally looked as if he was. He had bunches and bunches of crumpled up money shoved into a stack of rusty old biscuit tins in a tall kitchen cupboard. He said he'd had no reason to sort things when there'd been no visitors in the house, but now that I was here, it was time he pulled himself together.

I said there wasn't any need to go to any trouble on my behalf, but he said, "No, no, I must bite the bullet. You are my lucky omen and I must respond accordingly."

It was astonishing that anyone could think of me as lucky, but I liked that he did. He ordered a dumpster and he started to get rid of a lot of stuff.

He lit the fire, which filled the whole place with black smoke.

He said it felt good to be straightening things out. He said that Peggy would have hated to see him taking such poor care of everything. Peggy had been his wife but she was dead. There were pictures of her all over the place. She had curly hair and in all her pictures she was smiling and her cheeks looked lovely and round.

"She has a very nice face," I said, and he nodded a few times and without looking at me hurried into the kitchen mumbling something about having to make tea. And I let him go off to the kitchen on his own—sometimes people are not able to show their sadness to other people.

Newspapers, yellowed and curling, were stacked to the ceiling in the hallway. The kitchen was caked in substances so solid that it was impossible to say what they might have once been.

Every door that I opened revealed the same thing. Loads and loads of rubbish, teetering so dangerously it would be hazardous to walk around in case I was submerged in an avalanche of debris.

Although Barney was keen to get things cleaned up in my honor, there were lots of things he didn't want to throw out. It looked like he hadn't got rid of a single object or scrap of paper since around 1963. That's what you get for living in the past, is what he said.

It took us a while, but Barney said we could use the "storage room," which was really a room full of rubbish, and slowly we made progress, agreeing together that dirty wads of paper that had been fused together by damp and age were not useful to anyone and could be dumped. After he had done that, he said it was a weight off his mind. Peggy would have killed him for letting things pile up the way they had.

Homer, who'd been suspicious at first, barking every single time he added something to the dumpster, eventually calmed down. Homer got into the habit of sleeping on my bed that we'd put together from cushions and blankets and pillows. When Barney disappeared during the nights, Homer stayed with me and any time I moved, he'd wag his tail as if to tell me he was glad I was there and to remind me that he wasn't going anywhere.

In a shelf between two books, I found an old scrap of paper with a recipe called "Peggy's lemonade" and I said that looked great. Soon he was coming home every night with bags, and in the morning I'd see that he'd bought things like brown sugar and lemons as well as the ingredients I'd asked him to get for apple tarts.

An old shed was buried right at the back and we'd pulled out the rusty mower and it had taken a while, and I'm not saying we'd have won a tidy-garden competition, but things got slightly neater and tidier and less jumbled and scrambled and not quite as much of a mess—and the dumpster got filled up with rubbish.

Every so often, Barney would try to suggest that people might be missing me, and that this was no place for a boy in need of help, but I told him it was perfectly okay.

"I can't go home," my voice said every time he talked about how people must be frantic about my disappearance. I wished things were simpler. I wished I could go back to my window and lean out and chat to Meg the way I used to. Part of me thought about myself walking out of Barney's and down the long hill and back into my house the way he was suggesting. But some people can't come home, and the reasons are never simple or easy to explain and when I told him that he said he knew what I meant.

I told Barney about my dad and how since my mum died he'd got quieter and quieter until it seemed to me that he stopped saying anything. Over the years my dad had slipped into the gray silence that I'd often remembered wondering if he was ever going to come out of.

It had taken a while for my dad to undergo this metamorphosis, but by the time it was complete his old friends had to look twice before saying hello to him in the street. People stopped recognizing him in shops, and even my teachers went, "Is that your dad?" when they saw him standing in the school yard waiting for me in his limp-looking coat. It was embarrassing.

Later when I started secondary school and could cycle home by myself, Stevie didn't see any improvement. When he went to pick Stevie up, Dad wouldn't talk to anyone else, not even when people said hello. He stood, hands in pockets, not noticing even when rain had started to fall and even when it was dripping off his nose and his chin and his earlobes.

"Right then," Barney had said, "we will have to write a list, and you, young man, are going to have to make a plan." I didn't want to make a plan—I didn't know of any plan that was going to get me out of the situation I was in, but I did say I'd keep helping him with the house and I thought that was a relatively good start considering what a bad state of mind I'd been in not so long ago. And I hoped that we could keep on doing stuff to clean up and that I'd make myself so useful he'd forget about coaxing me back home.

I told him about how the car my dad had bought after the accident had, over the years, got louder in inverse proportion to Dad's growing silence. It used to drive me mad. Clattering home on account of the exhaust being loose, and Dad not saying a single word.

I'd tried to get him to talk. I thought if I did, then maybe the cloud that followed him around might lift. I hardly remember my mum's face, even though Dad did his best on that front. Instead of reading me stories before I went to bed, he would sit with the same big book every night. It had no words in it. It was just full of photos of my mum. And I began to think that the inside of my dad was exactly the same: no words. Only pictures of her. Silently he would turn the pages until he got to the end, and then he would kiss me on the forehead and turn off the light. Pictures of your mum are not the same as your mum. I couldn't remember the smell of her, or how she looked when she walked into a room, or what her voice sounded like. All I remembered were the photographs—flat, still, shadowy things.

I did my best with my dad. I was forever thinking up things to say to him, stuff that might have made him laugh. Funny things that had happened in school, interesting information the teacher had taught us, strange questions about the state of the world.

It seemed to me that when Dad had lost my mum, he'd also lost his voice. On the plus side, he became amazingly tidy. Like a ghost, he would move silently around the house, keeping things in order.

I ended up telling Barney practically everything—not just about Meg's letter and Paloma and Dad and his silence and Stevie, but about other stuff too. And because of the no TV and no Internet in Barney's house, talking was the thing we did most. Barney was a smoker, which I wasn't too keen on and when I told him, he was all apologetic and sometimes he used to excuse himself after tea and I'd watch him standing out in the garden with a cloud of smoke surrounding him like a halo.

I hadn't wanted to talk about the apple-tart fiasco, but, as I might have mentioned before, Barney was a listener.

The TV crew had done an advance visit to our school to plan everything. They were looking for stories of ordinary kids doing amazing things.

"That boy has talent dripping from his fingertips," Mr. O'Leary had said after I'd brought a tart in one day for no other reason than because my dad had broken his normal silence to suggest that I should. And I was to demonstrate to everyone how I made them and they were going to make it into a show. The funny thing was that I didn't even really want to do it. I kept on telling them it was an ordinary, unremarkable thing and I wasn't too sure if anyone would even be that interested. I kept telling them that they should look for someone with a more obvious talent to take the slot. But they wouldn't hear of it. And they insisted, and so the cameras were scheduled and signs went up in school, and Paloma didn't say that much to me about it, not after the decision was finalized.

Her mother came into the school and was a bit loud talking to Mr. O'Leary in a booming voice right in front of everyone. She'd said, "What are you thinking? My daughter is among the most talented children in the entire country and this would be the perfect opportunity for her and instead you're giving the slot to some nerdy kid who's obsessed with cooking? Come on, you and I both know that's not the kind of thing that's going to put this school on the map. In fact it's not the kind of thing that will do anything except to shine a rather odd light on you. And you have this glorious girl sitting right in front of your face? Come on? Have a bit of sense."

Mr. O'Leary had asked Paloma's mum to leave because she was not entitled to talk like that but everyone had heard and once something is said, nobody can pretend it hasn't been said. You can try to pretend, but it stays in everyone's head.


"Pastry from scratch—butter and flour and sugar, kneaded slowly, with cool hands. Bramley apples, skinned and carefully sliced, with an extremely sharp knife—never cut apples with a blunt knife; you might as well use a spoon—the pieces must be crisp and flat. Cinnamon crushed directly from bark, nutmeg sprinkles, brown and pungent grated straight off a whole nutmeg."

It was what my gran had taught me.

"You need patience and you need skill and you need to get into a particular state of mind, but without the right ingredients, there's not much point in even starting. You might as well go off and do something else."

Whispers and rustles floated in the air. Andy and Greg made fart noises from the back of the class even though they were in the middle of recording the whole thing. Paloma did her languid, slow-lidded blink. And some of the others like Christina Bracken and Paul Campion snapped their chewing gum and stared menacingly at my demonstration.

"Apple tart? Oscar, that's weird," somebody said from the back row, but I continued with my demo, and Mr. O'Leary kept saying, "Shush, shush everyone, please give Oscar some respect and attention." As if that was going to make any difference because once a class of people has decided to turn on you, you can't do much about it.

"Go on, Oscar, please continue."

"To be able to mingle different kinds of food into one single delicious thing is a kind of alchemy. Not everyone appreciates that."

"No indeed," said Mr. O'Leary, glaring at the rest of the class, "not everyone does."

"A normal-sized apple tart should easily be enough for six people." I kept going. I didn't want to wreck the recording, and I'd started so I wanted to finish.

"The butter should be pale yellow and fresh and unsalted. The sugar needs to be the brown, almost moist kind that slowly tumbles over itself when you spoon it into the mix, like so. See?

"Even after they're cooked, the apples should have a bit of bite to them. The pastry has to be extremely light so that it melts the moment it's in your mouth. If you take the time it needs, and if you concentrate properly, what you'll end up making is this!"

I pulled out a tart I'd prepared earlier.

"Ah, Oscar, that's very good, that's very good indeed. Now let's hear a bit about your influences? Your inspiration? The people who taught you this skill."

In my mind I saw my dad's photo album of my mum and I thought about her mum too, who was my gran, and I got filled up with sadness the way you sometimes do when you're not expecting it. But I kept going:

"In everything you do," I tried to explain, "you need to respect the integrity of things, especially when you're cooking. Ingredients should always have a hint of their former selves, that's what my gran used to say. She's dead now but I remember everything she taught me. She made me practice for years and years, and even though I was quite a small kid, she never let me off the hook.

"'Oh that's not it at all,' she'd say the first few times I tried.

"And then later, 'Better than the last time, I'll grant you that,' and eventually, 'Oscar, I daresay you've almost got it!'

"I finally did get it right, of course, because I kept on trying and I didn't allow myself to be discouraged. I knew I'd done it, even before my gran told me—as soon as I lifted it out of the oven, I could see by the look of it—golden and toasty and spicy and hot— that I'd made the grade. My gran asked for her special silver fork and when she tasted the tart, she clapped her hands and she looked into my eyes and she said, 'Oscar, my darling boy!'

"An hour later, she was dead. Too much joy in the body of a frail woman can apparently be fatal. That's what my dad had said."

I could hear loud laughs from the back of the room.

"I can't really stand it," I could hear myself saying, my voice so low because part of me didn't want anyone to hear, "the way everyone has to die or go away in the end. I can't stand it the way I think it was probably me who killed my gran, even though everyone said I didn't, but on the other hand, I find it quite comforting that her final moments were sweetened by brown sugar, spices and the taste of perfectly cooked apples."

The class was silent now but the boys were holding their hands over their mouths. I looked around the room. To finish up as quickly as possible I said, "Thank you, the end, thank you very much."

And after that, the whole class just burst out laughing, and I walked slowly out of the room, grabbing Andy and Greg's camera on the way, not looking at anyone. I took the memory card out of the camera and flushed it down the toilet.

Paloma wanted to run after me, she told me later, but she wouldn't have been able to say anything and I could hear Mr. O'Leary saying, "Be *quiet* everyone. Nobody is to *move*, while I go and talk to Oscar. Do you hear me?" Paloma told me that before Mr. O'Leary left the room, he told Andy and Greg that they were not to attempt to pursue me for their precious memory card. Andy and Greg had a race then up to the front where apparently they pulled apart my apple tart and they stuffed it into their mouths. Paloma said she had told them to stop and to leave some for me, but they ignored her.

"He wants us to eat it," they'd said. "Why do you think he went to the trouble of making it?" It was completely gone by the time I came back.

After that, I sat through the whole of double math, looking straight ahead at the wall, not looking at anyone or saying anything when Mrs. Fortune asked questions, even though I knew the answers.

Later when we were walking home together, Paloma told me I should do my best to try to forget about the apple-tart humiliation.

I looked at her and kind of out of the blue, I really did see then what everyone else had been talking about. I thought that maybe if I could kiss her, that would be a good way for me to forget about Meg and the apple-tart incident and everything.

And when we reached the corner before turning into our houses, that is what I tried to do. I tried to kiss Paloma Killealy. But she turned her face away from me and she said:

"Oscar, it's too late. Timing is everything. I gave you your chance but you blew it. Paloma Killealy only ever gives people one chance. You're not going to get another just because you've changed your mind. Oscar, sorry, but that's not the way it works in my world. And, anyway, things are changing Ratio-wise too. I thought you were one of the alpha boys when I first got here, but now? Now of course we all know you're not. I could only ever go out with someone on the A-team, if you know what I mean."

I know it sounds like she might have been vain, but look, at the time, I thought she had a point. She was the one who knew about The Ratio, not me. And it wouldn't have done for her to have made some terrible mistake as she was trying to settle in, what with me and my apple tarts and so on and how the class had kind of stopped understanding me. I understood that.

I asked her if we could still be friends, and she was like, Of course, Oscar, sure we can, but here's what I'm suggesting: let's stay friends, but when we're at school, let's give our friendship a lower profile, okay?

It didn't really occur to me then that friendship shouldn't have conditions like the ones Paloma was suddenly insisting on. If you're a friend of someone outside school then you should be a friend of theirs inside school too. But she was pretty firm about it so I said, "Fine Paloma, whatever you think."

Barney said that as far as he was concerned, friendship either is or it is not. It should never have qualifications—it should never need to be explained or excused.

"Are these the reasons you wanted your life to be over, Oscar?" Barney had asked then. And I'd said no. And he said I should be aware that the town was developing its theories about me, and how most people would probably think it was because of the beautiful girl. And I said, "What do you mean?" and he said the world loved to believe that boys killed themselves because of beautiful girls who didn't love them and I said it wasn't that. It was something else.

"It's the thing that happened that means I can never go back."

"Would you like to tell me about it?" he said gently, but again he said that there was no pressure. And I said that yes I would.

A few nights before the apple-tart demo, Paloma's mum had come over to introduce herself to my dad and she was seriously all *over* him. And at first he hardly looked at her and hardly said a word even when she asked him tons of questions, and I'm secretly thinking, Dad, can you just please behave like a normal person. But the second time she called, Dad was a little bit chattier, and the third time he mentioned afterward that she seemed like a very nice person.

But, Barney, I can tell you now, I never really liked the look of her. She used to do this big sigh every time she saw Stevie as if he was the saddest sight she'd ever come across.

"Was he born in a wheelchair?" she'd asked as if he wasn't right in front of her.

"No," I'd answered helpfully, "he wasn't. I think you'll find that nobody is born in a wheelchair. You get a wheelchair if you need one, after you're born." And she thought this was the most hilarious thing she'd ever heard because she laughed for much longer than someone should laugh at anything really.

So then she said, "Bill, you must come over to dinner," but Dad says no really, thanks very much and everything, but I don't like to leave the boys in the evenings. And she said, "I know!" as if she had the biggest brainwave of all time. "I'll bring dinner over here! Just name the night and I'll do the rest!" And my dad mumbled something under his breath and then said, "Okay, then, give me your number and I'll text you."

This turned out to have been the biggest mistake ever, because she insisted on getting his number too and every day for a week she texted him. Eventually even he realized it was impossible for him to keep ignoring her.

The following Friday she barged in with dinner for everyone. She did most of the talking. She even did the washing up, and just when we thought it was all over, she invited herself back again. And there was hardly any mention of Paloma except to say that she was studying, which is something I'd never seen Paloma doing—either at school or at home.

So then next time, Mrs. Killealy brought two bottles of champagne with dinner, and Dad was so nervous he drank it the way you might drink water if you were extremely thirsty, and they talked and talked and talked for the whole night.

She had some strong opinions about how to run a business:

"The only way to get ahead in life is to annihilate your rivals. Blow them out of the water. Sweep them away by whatever means necessary, that's the trick."

She sparkled with diamonds from her ears and her neck and her fingers. And she clamped her teeth together in an aggressive smile, and she nodded her head as she stood behind my dad and her bony fingers grabbed him by each shoulder and she squeezed them.

She snarled when she spoke and whenever she made a point, she leaned over and peered into my dad's eyes and banged her bony fist on the table for emphasis so that the pepper pot shook.

And the sun, I swear, was coming up when she finally left, and I don't know what they talked about but I do know that Dad was crying. Crying in front of Paloma Killealy's mother who, it turned out, is divorced, not that Paloma ever told me anything about that. It was obvious by now that she was throwing herself at my dad.

And, at first, I thought how awful that was, but then I started to believe that maybe it could be a good thing. My mum had been dead for a long time. By now my dad had been talking more to Mrs. Killealy than I'd remembered him talking to anyone for years. I didn't find out exactly what they'd been talking about until after I tried to kiss Paloma, but then Paloma told me. You see, Barney, there's something about my mum's death that I never knew, and now that I do know, I can't go back and you can't force me.

Barney said he wouldn't dream of forcing me to do anything, that I had to do things of my own free will, and I said thanks.

# the seventeenth slice

When you grow up by the sea there's a kind of magic that never leaves you. The shimmery silver of salty mornings stays inside your bones. The rattling of windows on a winter night sharpens your senses. There's always power and deceptiveness in a flat blue sea. I'm a coast-town girl. I know how quickly gentle water can turn into a black foaming mountain.

It couldn't have been coincidence, like some people said. Paloma Killealy had definitely been avoiding me. I tried again and again to confront her. I had a shed load of questions to ask. I needed to talk to her about the time she'd spent with Oscar, and the rumors that had been spread about him, and maybe get to the bottom of everything that had happened. I kept on scurrying around the school looking for her, and that day after finishing my session with Katy Collopy, I saw her slender legs hurrying out of the school gates, and her hair doing that swishing thing it always does.

I was sick and tired of trying to get a hold of her. After school I texted Stevie and told him I was just about to call into her house.

Well, it was my house to be precise, but I wasn't living in it. I knocked on the door with my fist, and then I hammered on it. And then I could hear that familiar noise of my own front door opening, and there was Paloma.

I couldn't understand what the expression on her face meant: her lips were pressed together, her forehead puckered and her eyes half open as if she was squinting at a very bright, low sun. She stepped forward and put her arms around me.

"Oh Meg!" she said in a half whisper. "I'm so *grateful* to you for coming. You are so kind to come here to show your support at this difficult time. I want you to know how much I appreciate it."

I'd been expecting a lot of things from my first meeting with Paloma Killealy, but the two things I hadn't been expecting were affection or gratitude.

And then she was taking me by the hand as if I was a small child, and leading me into my own kitchen and inviting me to sit on one of my family's kitchen chairs, at the table that me and Oscar had scratched our names on the bottom of when we were small. And I was saying,

"Please, Paloma, please, tell me what happened to him."

My phone began to ring but I turned it off.

It was like being hypnotized and it felt funny being a stranger at my own table. She had a lovely smile and looking at it, I couldn't imagine her ever wanting to do any harm to anyone.

She told me about how she'd done her best. She'd tried to protect him from other people's bad opinion of him.

"I did my best to explain a few basic ground rules—ones that he hadn't been able to pick up on his own. I thought I could give him some feedback, steer him in the right direction. But he didn't do himself any favors. He used to make apple tarts. I mean seriously, who does that? What other boy do you know goes around baking things in their spare time? That's not normal. Andy and Greg recorded this very silly apple-tart demonstration and him talking about his dead relatives, because they wanted to put it on YouTube. I told him that I reckoned he needed to give up the apple tarts. I told him it was too unusual. I thought I was doing him a favor."

Paloma asked me if I'd like to join her in the living room and then she showed me the way as if I didn't know where it was. We stood in front of the fire for a bit, and she kept talking about how attached she had been to Oscar, and how she forgave him for his weirdness, and what a good friend he had been in other ways, and how much she missed him and how she really did hope that it wasn't her fault.

I hated myself and I hated my jealous, horrible heart. What was the point of being jealous of her now? She was beautiful. Oscar had been right about her having hair like golden silk. Her skin was so soft it glistened. It began to seem to me as if none of this was her fault. I didn't want to bother her anymore. As I was about to leave, and tell her how sorry I was to have troubled her, she gave a little cry and said:

"Oh Meg," and she sank into our sofa, and she began to sob.

"Tell me," I said, "what's making you cry like this?"

"Meg, you see the whole thing *is* my fault, and I've been living with it this whole time and I have no idea who to talk to about it, because you see, as soon as everyone knows, they'll think so terribly badly of me." She put her head in my lap and she began to sob and I stroked her golden silky hair and I felt sorry for her because she really did look so sad, and I asked her to explain.

"Oscar was desperately, deeply, and devastatingly in love."

"With who?"

"Who do you think?" She frowned a little and pulled her hair back from her face and stretched her long neck.

"I don't know," I said.

"With *me*, of course. I think I must have broken his heart. Because there was never going to be a scene between me and Oscar. Dunno if you've heard but Andy and me are a couple now and goodness, poor Oscar, look, I know he had a thing for me, it was obvious, but . . . I never thought the consequences would be . . . Meg, and then he started acting kind of weird. I began to see things about him too. I mean, he was really popular when I first came but you see it turns out that he was a weirdo. He freaked me out."

"What does that mean?"

"He used to *look* at me—in my bedroom. He used his telescope to try and get close-up views. He invaded my privacy. But look, I understood. I forgave him."

"You're making that up. Or you were imagining it. That doesn't sound like him. Not the Oscar I knew."

"Yeah, well ask anyone. It wasn't just me. Loads of people had started to think he was strange."

"People? What people?"

"Andy and Greg mainly, but others too. I tried to teach him. I tried to help him Meg, I honestly, truly did."

A wave rippled through me as if a cruel wind had started to blow.

Everyone might be right after all. Oscar really might be dead. Dead from obsessive love for a girl who didn't love him back.

When I got up to say good-bye, we hugged again in the doorway. I felt comfort and warmth. She even smelled beautiful. Strawberries, almonds and roses were the kinds of things that Paloma Killealy smelled of. Good smells, and pure smells and things that it was difficult to be suspicious of.

But before I turned to leave, I could feel a shiver of something swimming around between us. Something secret. Something cruel.

When I got home I switched on my phone again and saw seven missed calls from Stevie, so I rang back.

"Meg!" he whispered. "Look, I'm sorry to be ringing you so late but I need to tell you something. It's about Oscar. He's not dead, Meg. He never died!"

"What?" I whispered back. "How do you know?"

"Because," said Stevie, "he's been in contact!"

I held my breath for a few seconds.

"In contact with you?"

"Yes!"

"How?"

"I leave notes for him, down at the pier. In the beginning, I didn't have a proper system. I'd put a lot of important things down on those bits of paper. Things I wanted him to tell me, or things I wanted him to know. But they all fluttered away in the wind out to sea. So I stopped for a while, but for the last few days I've been writing some more, and pinning them down at the bottom of the wall with a rock. Each time I checked, the notes hadn't been moved. I was starting to lose hope. But tonight! When I went down there, all the notes were gone!! He's been back, Meg. He's here somewhere. He took the notes. Finally we have proof. Isn't it fantastic?!"

It was hard not to have hope. It would have been great if Stevie had been right, and for a second, I believed he was. I wanted to. Of course I did. Who wouldn't? I pictured Oscar at the pier again, picking up Stevie's sweet notes and reading them, and I too could feel a rock load of weight lifting off me.

But then something else happened. Big tears tumbled onto my face, splatting the glass on my bedside table with transparent shiny little sunburst shapes.

"Stevie, it's late. Let's talk about this tomorrow," I said. And to the sound of Stevie talking, breathless and delighted, I turned off the phone. If Oscar had seen any kind of note from Stevie pinned down like that at the end of the pier, he wouldn't have stayed away. It just didn't make sense anymore. An icy new feeling seeped over me. I threw my phone across the room, as if it was a bomb that was about to explode, but it just landed on the middle of my bed with a blunt thump.

Katy Collopy had been right. Stevie was in the grip of some kind of deep denial on account of how much he wanted Oscar to be alive, and Stevie's hope was strong and it was as solid as a real object. My own hope was disappearing now, like something else had begun to die.

It was because of the things Paloma had told me. Stevie kept willing his lovely brother to be with us, but we had to accept that Oscar was gone. And it was because of Paloma and how beautiful she was and how Oscar had fallen in love with her. It wasn't her fault that she didn't love him back. You can't help the way you feel. But the way he felt had been the thing that destroyed him. And now, the thought of him hurling himself off the pier seemed to have a logic to it that I'd never understood before.

I found myself facing the fact of Oscar's death for the first time. It was like stumbling upon the foot of a stairway that I'd never noticed, and not being able to stop myself from walking relentlessly to the top.

Soon after that, Paloma and her mother got in contact with my parents and said they would be vacating our house earlier than planned. My parents said how thoughtful this was of them and they hoped we weren't putting them out and they said not in the slightest, it was the least they could do and anyway they'd found somewhere "quite marvelous" to live.

Paloma's mum had bought a five-bedroom house, even though she had only two people in her family. It was near the park. People said they had a tennis court in the back garden and an underground swimming pool.

\* \* \*

At school, everyone seemed to have stopped talking about Oscar completely. I'd gone in early one day to rub the graffiti off his locker, but when I got there, the graffiti was already gone because his locker door had been pulled off, and someone must have cleared out whatever was in it because there was nothing there.

And I thought being back in my house was going to be helpful. I imagined it would make me feel normal and calm, but it didn't. For one thing, I couldn't bear to sleep in my room with Oscar's window blank and silent in front of me. I didn't even have to explain. My parents let me put the blow-up mattress in the living room, right up against the wall closest to Stevie's room. I could see his candle, flickering and quivering away, never going out.

I whacked an old branch on Stevie's like Oscar used to on mine, and I saw his shadow coming to the ledge and his smile reminded me so much of his brother that I thought it was possibly going to break my heart.

Stevie's dad stopped me on the way to school one day and said how much he appreciated me keeping the "tradition of the windows" going and how much I was doing to keep Stevie cheerful and happy. It felt good—a bit like being a big sister maybe, keeping an eye on him like that, trying to get him to realize the terrible thing that had happened to his brother without letting it destroy him. I reminded Stevie about Paloma and how lovely she was and how much Oscar had liked her and I thought he was making sense of it too, and that it would be good for him. And we talked at the windows and I said to myself, if Oscar's not coming back, at least I can mind Stevie and look out for him because I'm sure that's what Oscar would have wanted.

And our chats were really good until the evening he came to the window and he said, Meg, you've been lying to me and I want you to go away and never talk to me again.

# the eighteenth slice

I told Barney how, totally by mistake, Paloma told me something about my mum who is dead. She'd heard about that whole terrible accident that killed my mum and hurt Stevie. And what she told me made me realize exactly how worthless I was.

In school, the day after I'd tried to kiss her, Paloma had called me over.

"Oscar, Oscar," she'd shouted right in the middle of the school yard, and I ran over to her and she asked me to tell everyone what I had wanted to do to her the day before. And, of course, that was private so I wasn't going to announce it to the rest of the class, but everyone had gathered around, and Paloma goes, "Oscar Dunleavy tried to *kiss* me last night, didn't you, Osc?" And a few people started to laugh. And I laughed as well because I didn't want it to get nasty.

So I laughed a bit more and so did she and then she leaned over and whispered in my ear. "See this, Oscar? Everybody's laughing at you now. You didn't honestly think that you and me were going to be, you know, that there was ever going to be an 'us'? That's not a possibility. That's never been a possibility." I told her that was fine with me, that seriously, she didn't need to keep going on about it, but Paloma never stopped talking until she was ready to.

"I was being nice to you," she continued. "And of course we can always be friends."

"You don't have to be nice to me if you don't want to," I said.

"Oh but I like being nice to you. On account of how brave I think you are."

And I said, "Brave? What do you mean, brave?"

And she said, "I mean courageous. I mean strong. I can only imagine how guilty you must have been feeling for your whole life."

"Guilty? Why should I be feeling guilty?" I'd asked her.

"Because of Stevie and your mother," she'd said, slowly. "I honestly don't know how you manage to stay so cheerful. You are resilient, Oscar—keeping going the way you've done since Stevie's accident. Guilt must be such a difficult thing to live with," she said, and the way she spoke was full of some kind of explosive meaning that I didn't yet understand.

"You know, seeing him every day in his wheelchair, and knowing, that's the awful thing, knowing that it's you who put him there."

"Paloma, what are you saying? It was an accident. A car accident. Someone crashed into us—it wasn't even the man's fault."

"It's always somebody's fault," she said, looking carefully at my face, and then she said, "Oscar, you don't have to keep the secret from me, because I know. My mum told me. She had this long conversation with your dad the other night. You poor thing, Oscar. That's a terrible burden to carry, and I just want to say maximum respect for being so okay about it, and for not letting it weigh you down."

I told her I'd be very interested to hear the parts of the story Dad had told.

So then she told me the story. The story of my family that nobody had ever bothered to tell me even though it turns out I'd played the main part.

"Your dad told my mum the bit about how he'd been keeping his sorrow to himself for a long time. My mother is good at getting information out of people. I've seen how she does it. Usually she keeps filling up their wine glass even though they don't want any more wine, and she gets them to tell parts of the story of their life that they've never told anyone.

"He told her the bit about how you and your family had been on the way to Galway, and how everyone was happy and excited because you were going to the beach. The sun was high in the sky because you'd started out late, and Stevie was strapped into his car seat and you were singing some song that you used to sing and you were only six but you were smiley and buzzy the way only six-year-old children can be, and your mum was driving. Your dad said he couldn't remember why it wasn't him who was driving. He explained the bit about how much you loved your brother, even then, when he was tiny, and he told my mum that Stevie must have been bored or maybe hungry or something, on account of you being late setting out. Your dad kept explaining to my mum that he should really have given you some lunch *before* you left but he was the one who insisted that you press on. And your dad is sure Stevie started to hold out his arms to you, because you said, 'Mum, Dad, Stevie wants to get out,' and your dad explained how he kept saying, 'No matter what Stevie does, do not let him out of that car seat, not until we find somewhere to stop.' I mean you *were* going to stop, but you were on the highway. You had to find somewhere, you see.

"He told her the bit about how your mum had kept on driving and he was reading the map and was distracted by something, and next thing he turned around and you have Stevie on your knee and the two of you have these huge smiles on your faces like you've done something really brilliant and you're delighted with yourselves. As soon as he looks at you, he lets out this gasp, you know, because of how it's so dangerous for a baby not to be strapped in. And then how your mum looked around and was equally shocked and took her attention away from the road and the car drifted across to the other side and hit a truck. The truck driver was devastated afterward, but it hadn't been *his* fault."

The whole time Paloma was telling me the story she was looking into my face.

I was dizzy. I was sick.

I wanted to find Meg. I needed to talk to her. But Meg wasn't my friend anymore. She didn't like me because I was an idiot. Everyone in my class knew it. Paloma knew it better than anyone. An idiot and a fool. An apple-tart-baking fool who killed his mother.

"I'm sorry," I kept whispering to myself for the rest of that day, even though I really should have been talking to Stevie. "I'm sorry for what I am. I'm sorry for what I have done."

Paloma was changing in front of my eyes. She was harder and tougher and meaner than I'd ever predicted, and I thought if I could only have a quick conversation with Meg, she might help me see straight.

But Meg didn't want to talk to me. Meg had moved on. There wasn't anybody I could turn to. Nobody who would listen or understand, and I panicked, Barney, because that's the kind of feeling that happens when suddenly you feel like you're on your own.

Lots of bad things were jumbling around inside my head. Everything kind of came crashing down. Does that make any sense, Barney?

Barney said that considering the things I'd told him, it made perfect sense.

"Oscar, my dear boy, I hope you understand that though you're welcome to be here, perhaps you need to rethink the strategy you've planned about hiding indefinitely. It might be wise to consider going home at some stage. You are feeling bad about something that you shouldn't be feeling bad about. And you'll realize that if you think about it. You need to talk to your father about all of this."

"No, I don't. I don't want to do anything anymore," I said, and I put my head in my hands again and I would not look at him or talk to him for a while.

Barney said, "All right, dear boy, perhaps you simply need a little more time."

"I don't need any more time. Time is useless. It's not going to make anything better, no matter how much of it goes by."

"Why did you let Paloma talk to you and treat you the way she did?" he asked me. "It sounds to me as if she was being quite unpleasant, quite mean, quite deceitful."

"Oh maybe she was, I'm not sure. I don't think she meant any of it. I just wanted to be friends with her. I didn't want any fighting. I wanted to keep the peace."

"I may be a fairly dim-witted old man," Barney said to me then. "But it seems to me as if that girl set out to make you feel terrible about yourself. One thing I've learned about peace is that not all of it is good. Peace can be fragile and peace can be ugly and peace can be wrong. Peace built on lies is no peace at all."

# the nineteenth slice

I got to the bottom of why Stevie suddenly didn't want anything to do with me. It took me days of pestering. He'd told me to go away, but I wouldn't. I kept on calling, and I kept on whacking his window, and in the end I wore him down. "Why, why don't you want me to talk to you?" I kept asking, and I was never going to give up because I didn't want to lose Stevie in all of this too. So at last, he told me.

"Mr. O'Leary from your school called around here the other day. He wanted to give us a package of things that had been in Oscar's locker. He thought it was stuff we might like to have. It was my chance to look through some of his things for clues and stuff. I thought it would be useful.

"But Dad said I wasn't to touch any of it, that he'd go through it when he was ready. He put it all away in a kitchen drawer . . . But he's my brother. I've a right to see the things he left behind. Anyway, guess what I found, Meg? What do you think I found?"

"I don't know," I said.

"I found a letter from you."

"Oh God, Stevie. Oh I'm sorry," I said, knowing what he was referring to, and seeing him hold up the envelope with my handwriting on the outside. "I'm just so mortified. You see, he wasn't ever supposed to read that, and anyway, I found out afterward that he didn't feel the same as I felt. Stevie, the whole thing was a total mess. I told him to ignore it. And he was glad that we were going to put the whole thing out of our heads."

"Anyone would have been glad to ignore a letter like this. What did you expect?"

"Honestly? Well, I guess once I knew he'd read it, I guess I kind of hoped that he'd feel the same way too. I dunno, I suppose part of me expected him to agree with me, you know? Have the same feelings."

"How could you have expected him to feel the same as that, Meg?" said Stevie and it looked as if he was going to cry, and the hope that I had always seen in his face looked as if it had deserted him now too. "How terrible you must be feeling now that things have turned out the way they have."

"Yes, it's another thing that I wish hadn't happened."

Stevie's face had crumpled then.

"Meg, how could you? How could you have said those things to him at the time when he needed your friendship most?"

"I know, Stevie, my feelings for him changed—it's hard to explain and maybe you're too young to understand."

Something suddenly wasn't adding up about Stevie and the way he looked so annoyed and I stopped and looked at the envelope he held tightly in his hands.

"Stevie, can you show me the letter?"

"Why?" he said, and his teeth were clamped together and he was not looking at me.

"Why do you want to see it again? You know what's in it. You know the words you typed—even if you didn't want him to read them, you still typed them."

"*Typed* them? I didn't type them, Stevie, I wrote them."

He did look at me again, then, and I looked at him and we both kept glaring at each other, fuming and silent.

"Stevie, please, show it to me."

Stevie smoothed the envelope. He handed it to me. I took it. I lifted the puckered lip, pulled out the note and opened it up. It had been folded and unfolded many times. I read what it said, and what it said was *nothing* I had ever written and nothing I would ever write and nothing I believed and nothing I would ever say. When I'd finished reading my shaking angry hands made the letter tremble between us.

I examined the envelope for signs of tampering—it had definitely been opened and closed a few times. Two little giveaway jagged vertical rips were on the lip. Someone had taken my letter out, replaced it and written my name at the bottom— though it was a careless and bad forgery because my handwriting was nowhere near as tall and liquid as the signature I was now looking at with my own eyes.

"Stevie, I swear to you, I swear I never wrote this."

Stevie's knuckles and his face had gone white and his lips were pressed together. He looked confused, so I started talking slowly to him to make sure he'd understood.

"I'd never have written anything like this to your brother; do you hear me? Someone took my letter—the one I wrote, and put this one in its place."

I held it up, then, away from my face as if it could do more damage than it had already done.

"Who could have done something like that?" whispered Stevie.

In a cold, clear instant I knew exactly who.

"It was on purpose, don't you see, Stevie? Paloma went after your brother. I think she wanted to destroy him."

"But I don't understand," said Stevie. "Why would she do that?"

"To keep me away from Oscar, maybe. To keep Oscar away from me? Because she's pure nasty and mean? To make him feel alone and unloved and abandoned and foolish and humiliated?"

Anyway, if they were the things that she had set out to do, I was afraid that she had succeeded.

"It's her fault," I said to Stevie. "Paloma Killealy. She did it to him, and the whole time she was pretending to be his friend."

"What could she have had against him?" he asked.

"His magic. His kindness. His charm. She was jealous of him and it was because Oscar had shone like a star and she wanted to be the one to shine. And she was furious with him for not being in love with her, because Paloma thinks the world should fall at her feet. And she was raging because Oscar did not. She wanted to dismantle him and take him down. And she thought about it and planned the whole thing with a whole lot of vicious intelligence.

"She purposely turned everyone against the idea that making apple tarts was a good and worthwhile, decent thing to do. She went around whispering things about him. Lies and innuendos that made everyone think he was weird. And she turned everyone against him and I hold her a hundred percent responsible for what has happened, but it was my fault too, Stevie.

"I mean, if anyone can save you from jumping off a pier, it's someone who's supposed to be your friend, don't you think? That's one of the basic reasons *for* friendship."

"Open the door, I know you're in there," I shouted until my throat was sore. When Paloma opened it, she stood in the doorway of her new huge house with the wind blowing her hair as if she was in a slow-motion movie clip, beautiful and perfect-skinned. I held the letter in front of her wide-eyed face.

"It's your fault," I said, "all your stupid fault. Why did you do it, Paloma? Why did you take my letter out and put a completely different letter in, one full of lies, pretending to be me? Why did you forge this and pretend it was from me and why did you humiliate him and why did you make him fall in love with you? And now he's gone! You have destroyed him completely, and you've taken him away from us—from his father whose heart is broken, from Stevie who only had one brother and whose mother is already dead, from me, who'll never have someone like that ever again, because there was only one Oscar Dunleavy. You are responsible for this.

"And now it turns out I had a chance! There was a chance he might have been for me, and I might have been for him and I'll never know, and I won't forgive you for it, Paloma Killealy. This is your fault. It will always be your fault."

She blinked slowly at me and looked sleepily into my face, unconcerned and blameless-looking.

"I have no idea what on earth you are talking about," she said. "Nobody can prove any of what you're saying. Now please go away. You're obviously out of your mind."

I'd planned to do her harm, though I hadn't thought through the specifics. But I realized there wasn't any point. My rage was strong and it made my body feel powerful, but it wasn't going to pull Oscar out of the deep. It was too late.

I couldn't make things better for anyone and I couldn't think what else to do, so I made an apple tart. It didn't come out the way Oscar's used to, but it was as close as I could get. I took it over to the Dunleavys and Oscar's dad hugged me and said I was a good person and how he knew I was only ever doing my best for Oscar, and Stevie came right over to me and hugged me around my knees too.

"Meggy, in case you think I've given up hope, I haven't. He's still not dead, he's alive, I keep telling you."

But Oscar's dad definitely didn't believe that anymore. I could see by the look on his face. He looked very tired. It must have felt better to give up. Hope can be exhausting.

"If you ever happen to be confused by something," Oscar always used to say, "it's a good idea to go to the sea. Things feel clearer when you're standing where the water meets the land and you can listen to the swell of the tide, and the pure enormousness of this ocean—huge and salty—connecting everything to everything else."

I know it's not a particularly normal thing to do—creep out of your bed in the middle of the night, and sneak away to go and sit on the end of a pier, but by now the squat bollard seemed to be calling for me practically all the time. I remembered how I'd told Katy Collopy about the whispering bollard, but how she hadn't been any help.

I knew that I wasn't suddenly going to find him or anything. But I needed to be on my own for a while, near to where Oscar had disappeared, when it was quiet and when no one would come and tell me to stop torturing myself or that enough was enough.

"Oscar, Oscaaaaar!" I knew that shouting for him wouldn't do any good, but still it made me feel better, there in the quietness.

Nobody can hear you from the pier. It's one of those funny things. I'm not exactly sure whether it's the way the harbor creates a cocoon of sound, or whether the sea has its own muffling effect, but it was something we had discovered long ago, me and Oscar. We could shout secrets to one another at that pier and nobody would ever be able to hear a thing.

"Oscar, where have you *gone*?" I shouted.

"Oscar, where are you *now*?" I begged.

"Why did you go without saying good-bye?" I pleaded.

"Oscar, I'm sorry," I screamed.

"Oscar, come back," I whispered.

I sat at the end of the pier dangling my legs over and looking at the water far below.

"I don't think he can hear you, from here," said a voice.

I rolled over and scrambled to my feet. A man was leaning, quiet and still, on the bollard.

I think I made some kind of startled noise, then. but I can't remember.

"I'm really terribly sorry to have disturbed you."

"Disturbed? What do you expect? Creeping up on someone like that in the middle of the night?"

"I don't wish to appear pedantic, but strictly speaking, it was you who crept up on me. I was here first." He switched on a flashlight and everything started to glimmer in its milky halo of light.

He was wearing a light suit. He looked smart, and his hands were beautiful and soft-looking.

He leaned over, staring at something else in his hands. He was rolling a scraggly wad of tobacco into a crinkly white rectangle of paper. On his little finger, a flat gold ring glinted. He licked the length of the small package, and stuck it down around itself, turning it, as if by magic, into a straight, tight, white stick. Such a nice delicate activity, except that in the end it was just a cigarette.

He cupped his hand around a box of matches that he'd taken from some inside pocket. There was that fizz and ripple that always happens when someone strikes a match. At the end of his cigarette, the dot of an orange glow sharpened and softened and sharpened again as he took a couple of drags.

I tried my best to act as if nothing in the world was bothering me. It's difficult to regain your composure when you've been seen shouting the name of your probably dead best friend into the inky blackness.

He didn't say any of the things you might imagine an adult would say when they come across a girl in her pajamas late at night. Nothing about what on earth I was doing, nothing about the risk of catching my death of cold, nothing about what my parents would say if they knew.

The night was windless and the sea was like a flat polished floor. From his cigarette, a tiny thin wisp of blue smoke tumbled into the sky.

"Please sit down again," he said. "I'm sorry for having made you jump like that."

Part of me was telling myself it would be wise to get away before I was murdered and dismembered, but his voice was gentle and vaguely recognizable, so I sat again on the ground so that I could feel the cold from the stone slabs seeping into me.

I put my elbows on my knees and I breathed in the salty air. And before I even knew what was happening, this sob burst out of me.

"My dear girl," said the man.

He didn't move or reach over or stand up. But his velvety gravelly voice was pure and good and the terrible tightness in me began to loosen its grip. Like a small key gently turning.

"What ails you?"

I told him that I'd been the friend of a guy called Oscar Dunleavy. I told him that I'd let my friend down very badly and that now he was dead and it was my fault.

"How is it your fault?" he asked. At first I couldn't answer. But when I started talking, I tried to explain how I'd deserted him when he must have needed me, and how my pride and my jealousy had stopped me writing to him and how now I would never be able to send him a message. Never again. I pressed my hands on the knobbly stone and I cried a good bit more.

"He was a friend of mine too," said the man, after I'd stopped crying and we'd been quiet for ages.

"Him and those legendary apple tarts."

I looked up, and it wasn't until that moment that I recognized him.

"Barney?" I said. "Barney Brittle? Is that you?"

"Yes," he said, and chuckled. "Indeed it is."

"But you're so clean!"

I apologized straightaway, because that could have been quite a rude thing to say, but he didn't seem offended. He smiled and said that things had got a lot better for him since he'd last seen me here.

"I'm a different man. The man you met was in a terrible place. Thankfully, not anymore. I have your friend Oscar to thank for helping me turn things around, and you too, Meg."

Barney said that the apple tart had been like a magic thing.

"People often ignore the misfortune of others, you see. The world is a heartless place but it's not always because they don't care. It's sometimes because they are embarrassed, or because they don't know what to say, or because they simply cannot bear to look into the eyes of someone who is suffering.

"Your Oscar had invented his own quite perfect response to people's troubles. As soon as he came across misfortune, he'd knuckle down to the only task that made sense to him at the time. He'd make one of those magnificent apple tarts."

For a few nights in a row, it seemed as if Barney could always be relied on. In the dead of night, he'd sit patiently on the bollard, with everything around him silent and hard to see apart from the orange glow of his permanently burning cigarette.

"Hello again, my dear," said Barney, and again it was as if we were meeting each other at a normal time in a normal place, not in the dead of night at the pier.

He told me he'd done a lot of things in his life but that recently someone had said that he was a good listener, and he'd realized that this was the thing he was probably most proud of now. Listening, he said, may be the most important skill you'll ever learn.

And it was true. He was really good at letting me finish whatever I started to say. Never asking stupid questions, but always encouraging me to go to the end of each story. Half a story is no good to anyone. And I don't know why, but explaining things to him helped me to understand them myself.

I told him about The Ratio, which was something that Paloma had tried to explain to me.

"It's the reason why people like Andy Fewer always get the girl with the perfect skin and the chocolate brown eyes and the hair like golden silk."

"Do you know what kind of a person she is?"

"Not really, I guess. I only know some things about her, but from what I do know, I think she's horrible. A horrible person with the face of an angel."

A little bundle of sticks and a log were bunched beside the bollard tonight, and on the other side, a purply suitcase sat scarred and pocked with age, a metal clasp glinting at its seam. Otherwise everything was pretty much the same as usual.

He rubbed his hands together and leaned over.

"You look as if you could do with some warmth," he said, opening the suitcase and unfolding a huge green blanket with one graceful gesture.

"Here, put this around you."

He lit a match under the nest of sticks. They crackled and popped for a second and then a great whoosh of light billowed into being. A seagull shrieked above one of the fishing boats and the wind made soft puckers on the surface of the sea.

My face got warmer by the fire and the blanket that had looked so light when he had tossed it across to me felt heavy around my body, pressing on my shoulders and my arms with its comforting weight, keeping me firmly planted on the spot.

"Meg, my dear" he said. "Is the loss of your dear friend weighing on you?"

"It's tormenting me," I replied. "In fact, I think it may be driving me mad. I came back because I was determined to find him. I came home refusing to believe what everyone else seemed to take for granted from the start. I've been searching for him, Barney, even when I don't mean to. I've been looking for his face in crowds, in corners, in places where he might have gone. I started my searching with so much hope, so much confidence, so much certainty, but my hope is running out now and I've almost forgotten what Oscar's face even looks like."

"That would be a tragedy indeed," Barney replied.

"Do you think I am missing anything?" I asked him, then, because he seemed so wise and so clever.

"Hmm," he said, "I'm not sure, but sometimes I sense things down here that could provide us with some kind of clue."

"What do you mean?"

"I get hints wafting up from the sea."

"Do you really?"

"Yes," he said, "things like grief, great loss and worry. Humiliation and guilt. And friendship and love and disappointment."

"Barney, do you have any idea what happened to him?"

"I can't answer that question but I will tell you a couple of things that I know."

I thought he was going to give me some information, something to go on, some lead to follow, but what he said was this:

"Nothing is as you think it is. Lots of things are not what they appear to be. Sometimes things look a certain way, but perhaps they are not.

Sometimes people need you to keep searching for them, or at least asking questions on their behalf. And very often, people have been silenced and they need other people to speak for them. It's when you stop searching and asking and speaking that they really will be lost. Don't give up, Meg."

"So you think he might be alive?"

"It's not what I think that matters," he said. He was being annoyingly cryptic, but it was good to talk to him and all of a sudden I found myself telling Barney about the letter.

"I wrote him a letter, telling him I basically loved him, but I've found out that Paloma switched it for a horrible letter that she wrote herself."

"Eh, Sorry? Excuse me? What did you say?"

I was in the middle of explaining it to Barney again—repeating how Paloma'd written a note and pretended it was from me. He was old and it seemed to me as if he might not have heard the first time.

"You loved him?" asked Barney. "You loved Oscar? Not just as a friend, but in the ancient way? The way that girls have loved boys for as long as there have been girls and boys?"

"Yes, what did you think?"

"And Paloma did *what* with your letter?"

I told him again.

"That venomous little vixen."

I told him I couldn't have come up with a better insult than that. And then he was struggling to his feet, putting out the fire and wrapping up his blanket, and suddenly he seemed to be in a terrible hurry.

"Dear me, Meg, I've remembered something. I need to be going, thank you I mean, good-bye, I mean, I must get back home, straightaway, I do apologize."

And before I could say another word, Barney was gone.

# the last slice

Barney was restless. His nighttime wanderings were starting to worry me. It got so that he never seemed to be able to sleep at night without getting up and heading off on some mysterious ramble or other. He would sigh, looking into the fireplace, and he would say "deary me" under his breath and I would keep on baking, but I was beginning to think that a thousand apple tarts couldn't cure the thing that Barney had.

So this one night, I stayed awake patting Homer on the head and wishing Barney was back. I was glad when I heard the clank of the gate.

"OSCAR! OSCAR! OSCAR!" He shouted as if he had something quite urgent to tell me and I went to the door and I saw him struggling up the hill like a man on a serious mission. He was standing at the gate leaning over. I waited, and he kept on standing at the gate, and then he held on to the pillar. I decided to go in and put the kettle on because there were still two slices of my last tart waiting for us and what could be more agreeable in the middle of the night—as he would say himself.

But Barney didn't come to the door. I kept on making the tea and putting the last two slices of tart on Peggy's plates, which have little pictures of lighthouses and sunsets on them. And suddenly, then, I felt afraid. I sort of knew that Barney was not going to come in, and I knew that something had happened to him and I could not bear it. I could not bear to go out to him. I just wanted to keep on making the tea and setting everything up nicely, because maybe if I pretended that nothing had happened, maybe if I kept on going on as if everything was completely normal and as if Barney was fine, then everything would be.

But Barney didn't come.

By the time I got to him, he was lying on the grass and I said, "Barney, Barney, please get up," but he couldn't. He could hardly even speak. He patted me on my head and I didn't know what to do. I asked him if he needed anything and he shook his head and all he'd say was, "My dear boy, it was a forgery!'

I'd no idea what he was talking about and thought he might be delirious or something so I said, "Don't try to talk, Barney, you're going to be fine."

I knew that if he wasn't going to be fine then this would be my fault too and I began to be really sure that I was the kiss of death. I wished that I had power and I wished I was strong but I was useless and I was weak and I killed the people I loved with apple tarts and stupid actions and not being able to bear to look.

I ran out of Barney's house, down the lane and I stumbled and I fell and I hurt my arm and hand and face. When I got up again, I kept running, waving my arms and saying, "Help, help, please help me, it's Barney Brittle. I think he's dying. He needs a doctor. We need to get him to a hospital fast. Somebody. Please. Help."

The ambulance men were really nice and they made Barney comfortable and they were patient, even though I asked them a lot of questions about what was wrong with Barney and whether he was going to be okay and whether or not it might have been bad for him to be eating quite as much apple tart as we'd been having recently. They said that they didn't quite know what was wrong, but that he was an old man and that even though he was impeccably dressed and obviously well-cared for, it was often hard to say how someone of his age might recover from an "episode" like the one he appeared to have had. They said poor Barney was a bit agitated and I wanted to sit beside him but they said that he needed specialist medical care.

"Dear boy!" he shouted again. "She never wrote that letter! She never wrote it. It was a forgery!" None of us knew what he was talking about and the more Barney tried to speak, the more urgently one of the nice ambulance people kept preparing something in a syringe, and then they plunged it into his arm and Barney's words melted into a low murmur and then he went to sleep altogether.

It was a relief to me on one hand, because I didn't want him to be distressed or disturbed or in pain, but the problem was that Barney breathing peacefully gave the two ambulance people a chance to focus on me.

"And who are you?" one of them asked me, to which I lied that I was Barney's grandson. They asked awkward questions then about the names of my parents and my siblings and whether I'd been staying with my grandfather alone and they were interested in lots of other things too. I wasn't going to get drawn into a discussion. I told them I was far too upset about Barney's health to be subjected to such an interrogation.

"Em, excuse me, but this is an ambulance. Can we please shift the focus back to the sick person?" The two of them said, "Yes, of course," but you could see they were looking at me suspiciously. I just stared very attentively at Barney, then, and inside my head, I begged him to be all right.

They allowed me to wait outside his room in the hospital and they promised they would let me in as soon as he was well enough to talk. I was totally delighted when I saw him next, because even though he was hooked up to monitors and tubes and stuff, he was cheerful and awake and he patted the bed and said I was to sit.

"Oscar," he said, "things might be about to change for both of us."

I said not to jump to any conclusions yet. This could be a small health hiccup and we could be back at the cottage before it got dark again.

He said possibly, but that we might have some explaining to do, and I knew he was right but I did my best not to think about it.

"I've been trying to tell you something—something you need to know. Your friend Meg—she wanted you to know that she was falling in *love* with you, and that's what she wrote in the letter, and that other . . . that so and so . . . that vixen of a girl, she ripped out those precious words from the envelope that Meg had put her letter in, and that, brat . . ." Barney began to cough and I had to give him some water even though I was starting to feel fairly numb, thinking about what he was telling me:

". . . that *brat* . . . replaced Meg's lovely words with other words, all untrue. Oscar, you simply must not let this misunderstanding prevail, do you hear me? This is your chance to clear everything up."

I didn't know if Barney really knew what he was talking about. Perhaps he'd imagined it, or had some vivid dream; they say that sometimes happens to the seriously ill.

"But Barney, you promised, you promised that I could stay with you in the cottage, and that you'd never ask me to go back."

"That was before *this*!" he said. "This changes everything and my promises are null and void. Meg wanted you to know that she loves you. My dear fellow, you must face everyone. Not just Meg, but your poor father and that little brother of yours and your friends and you must tell that awful girl, Paloma whatshername, that her behavior has been of the worst kind. She must know that you cannot attempt to damage people in the way she attempted to damage you."

"How do you know? How do you know about this?"

He told me how he'd met Meg at the pier. That's where he'd been going. He'd had whole detailed conversations with her about lots of things apparently, including Paloma.

"We got to know each other quite well. She's a terrific person," he explained.

"She's the one who told me about the Day of Prayer for you and how everyone was crying about you being gone, and so forth. She's the one who told me where Paloma and her mother are living now. Number two, The Paddocks—you know, on the other side of town."

I thought about Meg and how much I wished I could see her and explain everything, but it felt too late and I wondered how I could face anyone, especially her after what I knew about myself and the accident and all this pretending and hiding and this big massive lie that I had been telling the world.

"But Barney, what could I say to everyone? What could I say to Meg? How would I explain? How can I go back now?"

"How can you not?" said Barney, smiling at me.

He rummaged in his jacket then and pulled out a pile of wrinkled yellow notes.

"What are those?" I asked.

"They're messages from Stevie," he replied. I began to read.

"Excuse me, does your name happen to be Oscar Dunleavy?" asked a woman in glasses and a ponytail who seemed to have appeared out of nowhere. I supposed it was only a matter of time. I mean my photo had been everywhere, and there'd been a massive search and everyone knew what I looked like. I explained to Barney that if I was going back, I was going to do it in my own way. Ponytail lady's beeper went off and she scurried away. It was my cue. I kissed Barney's old hand, I stuffed Stevie's notes into my own pocket and I ran.

The rain was like a thousand little whips pelting at me from all angles. I leaned into the wind like one side of a triangle and I walked fast and steady, not stopping or hesitating or turning around because I'd decided by then and when you decide you should follow through.

I went to number two The Paddocks, and stood on the porch for a long time, looking at the details on the mailbox. I put my hand on the door for a minute or so, to get my balance. I told myself to stay strong even though I thought that as soon as I saw her, my new psychological might and wisdom would melt and I would be the Oscar I had been before, prepared to put up with anything for the sake of peace. But peace built on lies, I reminded myself, is no peace at all.

I stood on my toes and peered into the peephole.

Paloma was approaching and her face was distorted. Her nose looked massive —one eye huge, the other tiny.

I felt brave and that feeling is pretty much inked onto my brain now, like a permanent tattooed message that I will not forget.

I clamped my teeth together because they had started to

chatter, on account of me being so wet and pelted by the rain. The doorbell wasn't working. I tipped my finger at the flap of the mailbox and it swung and rattled back and forth pathetically, making a sound that probably nobody would hear. So I closed my fist and I hit the door with around ten bangs and I whispered Paloma's name and Paloma came. As soon as I saw her, a wind blew through me as if I was the door that had been opened. Her head was wrapped in a towel and her face had a white mask of cream smeared all over it.

"Paloma, it's me. I never died."

Her mouth opened for a second and then it closed and so did her eyes. She fainted like a bad actor from a movie, falling into a crumple of towel and cream and soft skin, and the towel miraculously stayed wrapped around her head like a turban. I picked her up. I had to. Nobody else was there.

"You replaced Meg's letter with a different letter, didn't you? And you were the one who made everyone think my apple tarts were lame and dorky? It was you, wasn't it? And you made up The Ratio because that's the way you want the world to work, but it doesn't have to work like that does it? And you knew I didn't know about the accident that killed my mum and injured Stevie and you told me about it on purpose, didn't you? You tried to break me, Paloma, but you have failed. I am not dead. I didn't kill myself."

"But, Oscar, someone had to show you things about yourself. You were a creep. You stared at me every night with that disturbing telescope. You stalked me inside my own bedroom."

"Paloma. I used that telescope to look at the *stars*. Why would I have used it to look at you?"

"Because I'm so beautiful," she said, a tense pulse beating inside her jaw.

I wanted to give her a chance to explain but nothing she said was plausible. She tried a different approach, then. She said she didn't know her actions were going to drive me to suicide.

"They didn't," I said.

"Why have you decided to come back?" she asked, tilting her head over to the side the way she always did.

"Love is the reason," I told her.

"Oscar, I like you a lot," she said, "I like you an awful lot more than everybody used to say. But I don't love you. I'm not in love with you."

"That's perfectly fine with me, because I'm not in love with you either."

"Then why did you try to kiss me that time?"

"Because I thought you wanted me to, and I was confused. But I'm not confused anymore."

"Then why are you here?" she asked, and I wondered how someone could be so deluded.

"I'm here because I have to tell you that it is wrong to do the things you tried to do to me. And you can go on pretending, but it's not going to make any difference. I'm here to ask you to tell me what Meg's letter said."

"Why don't you ask her yourself?" she said, and she tried to slam the door shut, but I put my foot in the way and I held it open.

"You work hard to make boys dream about you," I said to her. "Well, for your information, I don't dream about you. I dream about Meg.

"Boys falling in love with you makes you feel powerful and important, but it's a trick. I think you need to start thinking about other ways to feel good about yourself. That's my advice, Paloma, take it or leave it."

She thanked me and I said she was welcome and she said I was right and that I deserved someone better than her, which is a thing beautiful girls often say, regardless of whether it's true or not, but in this case she was totally right.

She told me that even Andy and Greg missed me, and I was like yeah right I really believe that okay, and she said, "No seriously, Oscar, it's true."

I'm not going to say too much about when my dad and Stevie saw me. What I will say is that first it was silent, and then it was loud, and then Dad cried and he kept saying "good grief," two words that shouldn't, when you think about it, go together.

Stevie came trundling out and did not look angry either. He hugged me around my knees the way he always used to. "I knew it," is what he said. "I told everyone, but nobody believed me!" he shouted, and he whizzed around and then hugged me some more, and I could feel the familiar scrawniness of his arms, only they weren't quite as scrawny as I remembered them having been. And he was talking fast saying stuff like, "Woo hoo. It wasn't a dream. I was riiiight I was riiiight!" and talking about the notes he'd left on the pier.

Amazingly, the three of us started to laugh. We laughed until we had to sit down on the grass in the front garden to recover.

I took his notes out of my pocket with the words of hope on them. They were short, full of encouragement and cheerfulness and I'm going to keep them for the rest of my life. They say things about how we need to keep going, and about never giving up and how valuable and good I am. Some of them ask questions, mainly about what are the things you need if you want to make a perfect apple tart.

Stevie and I talked for the whole day and into the night and Dad didn't stop us or tell us it was time to go to bed. We talked about life. I told him about how I had taken him out of his car seat when Mum was driving and that was why the accident had happened. And I asked him how he could ever forgive me and he said there was nothing to forgive.

We went outside and Stevie rolled around on the tarmac. "Listen, Oscar, and look at me, this *is* me now. If you're full of guilt because of something that couldn't possibly be your fault, that makes me feel like some kind of lame boy. I'm not a lame boy. In fact I'm pretty happy with myself," he said, and then he did a little twirl in his chair, spinning around and around and leaning backward and forward in a whole series of gravity-defying impressive moves.

"Watch me," he said. "See? Seriously, Oscar—who else in the world can do that? There are enough people who stare or cross the road or talk loudly to me like I'm a retard. Don't make me your sad secret, Oscar. I'm your brother, okay? Oscar? D'ya know what I mean?"

I did know.

And Stevie did his wheelchair moves and his chair shimmered in the light and sparks flew out from him as if he was made of moon drops, and as he twirled around they scattered around him, throwing a pale and beautiful reflection on his face.

I never really remembered that much about my mum, but my dad has begun to tell me about her. Apparently she was lovely. The most important thing about her was that she was kind. I think she must have learned it from my gran, who was extremely kind too.

Dad says kindness is magic. It looks gentle and mild on the outside, he says, but it has hidden powers. I know for sure that's definitely true. For example, it's still powerful enough to wake me up and have me jump out of my bed at weird times like three o'clock in the morning to make tarts.

You might think that eating apple tarts would be the last thing that someone would want in the middle of a crisis, but it turns out that the smallest forkful can make everything bearable again—even if the crisis is bursting with huge amounts of grief or if it's packed with massive loads of despair.

There've been journalists and TV guys and writers who've come especially to interview me about it, but when they ask me what the secret is, I shrug my shoulders because it's difficult to explain.

I realized I'd been avoiding her because I couldn't figure out what I was going to say. But I couldn't wait any longer. So the next night, I'm sitting at my window wondering what it's going to be like to be back at school and her light is on and then I can see her. It is Meg, of course, and she comes to the window and it's a bit like none of this has ever happened and it's just us again, because she doesn't say, "How dare you?" or "Where were you?" or "How could you?" and her face is soft.

"I need to talk to you," I say, and she goes, "You're talking to me now, aren't you?" And she is smiling. I tell her about the accident and what I did and she also says it's not my fault and the tears on her cheeks seem to make her face glow in the dark. And I'm feeling so many things at the same time that I can't breathe. Mainly that I never want Meg to feel sad. I want to take away all the sadness she's feeling now, and all the sadness she's ever felt and all the sadness she's ever going to feel, even though I know that I can't do that.

Then I tell her that the thing I need to say to her can't be said here at our windows. And she asks me what I mean, because we were always able to tell each other everything from here. But I tell her it won't do for the thing I have to say now. And I ask her to meet me by her gate.

"Be there in two minutes, then," she says. And she is, and before I have a chance to say anything, she puts her hand flat on the middle of my chest and she keeps it there for a long time. And though the future feels fragile and uncertain, the present has something new in it. Something sure.

Whatever waits for me tomorrow or next week or deep into the future, Meg's hand is right on the center of my body, still and flat and strong and small. I can't imagine anyone being more beautiful.

And if again I find myself on the end of a pier, thinking of jumping, or if I am again lost or desperate or if I feel I have nowhere to go, the imprint of Meg's hand is always going to be there, long after she has taken it away. It is going to be the thing that saves me.

I move my face down to hers and she moves her face closer to me and I say, "Is it okay?" and she says "Yes." I'm holding my breath when I kiss her. She closes her eyes and she kisses me back. I don't close my eyes. I keep them open so I can look at her close-up.

I still have lots of things to tackle of course, like my first day back at school, and Andy and Greg and the things that people might still be thinking or saying about me.

Right now, it's just Meg and me telling each other something that we both already know. We are alone, but I wish the whole world was watching. It is night, but already I'm wishing for the new day.